Ben carried he[r]

"Don't go," Sarah said. "Stay with me."

"Sarah, you don't know what you're saying. If I get into bed with you now...we're both too worked up, I don't know how much restraint we'd be capable of and I don't want to tempt fate. When we make love, *if* we make love, everything is going to be right."

She sighed deeply and lay back on the pillow. "You're right, Ben. I was panicked by a recurring dream I have. I wanted to stay awake and, yes, I wanted you. But I'm not free, am I? I may never be free to love you."

"Sarah, I...I'd better not say what I want to say, what's in my heart. Not yet."

And maybe not ever.

Not when Sarah Lasiter was still a married woman.

Dear Reader,

Be prepared to meet a "Woman of Mystery"!

This month we're proud to bring you another story in our ongoing WOMEN OF MYSTERY program, designed to bring you the debut books of writers new to Harlequin Intrigue.

Meet Paige Phillips, author of *The Tender Hours*.

Although new to Harlequin Intrigue, this author is no stranger to the world of publishing. She's written for a variety of publishers under a number of pseudonyms, including Kathryn Kent, Kathryn Sinclair and Amanda York. Primarily, she's written historical novels and is now trying her hand at contemporary romantic suspense with *The Tender Hours*.

We're dedicated to bringing you the best new authors, the freshest new voices. Be on the lookout for more WOMEN OF MYSTERY!

Sincerely,

Debra Matteucci
Senior Editor & Editorial Coordinator
Harlequin Books
300 East 42nd Street
New York, New York 10017

The Tender Hours

Paige Phillips

Harlequin Books

TORONTO • NEW YORK • LONDON
AMSTERDAM • PARIS • SYDNEY • HAMBURG
STOCKHOLM • ATHENS • TOKYO • MILAN
MADRID • WARSAW • BUDAPEST • AUCKLAND

ISBN 0-373-22372-2

THE TENDER HOURS

Copyright © 1996 by Joan Dial

Printed in U.S.A.

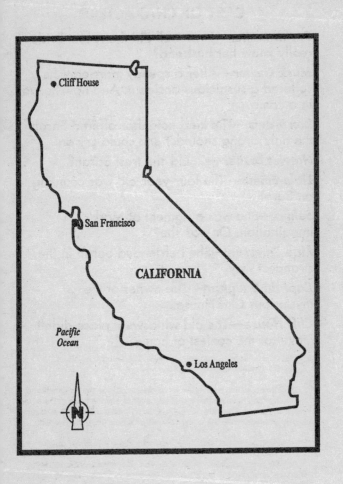

Cliff House

San Francisco

CALIFORNIA

Pacific
Ocean

Los Angeles

N

CAST OF CHARACTERS

Sarah Lasiter—How well did the recent bride really know her husband?

Mark Lasiter—After a speedy marriage, he suffered a suspicious accident. And now he was in a coma.

Ben Travis—The kind neighbor offered Sarah the only strong shoulder she could cry on.

Harriet Lasiter—Could she trust Sarah?

Little Emma—The four-year-old was counting on Sarah.

Selma—She was a figment of Mark's imagination. Or was she?

Mae Peterson—She befriended Sarah in the strangest way.

Captain Vaughan—The owner of the mysterious Cliff House.

Cliff House—The old windswept place didn't make for the coziest of homes.

Chapter One

The doorbell rang once, an urgent summons more compelling than repeated chimes. Jolted from shallow sleep, Sarah Lasiter sat up in bed, disoriented by the strange surroundings.

Glowing red digits on the alarm clock on the nightstand told her it was five past midnight. Outside the wind still howled and rain pelted the undraped windowpanes.

Listening, she waited for a repeat ring. Nothing.

Still, there *had* been that one ring. Had someone brought a message from the hospital?

Sarah jumped out of bed and grabbed her robe, wishing the telephone had been installed, wishing she was not alone in an isolated house with a four-year-old girl and an eighty-year-old woman.

The graceful circular staircase that had been so appealing a feature when she first saw Cliff House seemed less so shrouded in darkness. *First thing tomorrow,* she promised herself, *I'll replace the landing light bulbs.* Why hadn't someone thought to install a two-way switch at the top of the stairs?

Gripping the banister rail, she descended the stairs and, reaching the hall, turned on the light. She could see a blurred silhouette through the frosted-glass panel of the front door. Grateful for Mark's foresight in installing a dead bolt and chain before they arrived, Sarah opened the door a crack and peered out into the tempest-tossed night.

The woman standing on the rain-swept porch had long blond hair plastered damply to her head and straggling in sodden strands over the shoulders of a black leather jacket. Her black leggings and boots were mud spattered. She was model-tall, and in the dim light appeared to be in her late twenties.

"Is the doctor here? There's been an accident."

Taken aback, Sarah said, "How did you know there was a doctor—I mean—we just moved in today."

"Get him—please. A man's been hurt. Badly, I think."

"The doctor isn't here." Sarah wondered if she was issuing an invitation for robbers to appear out of the night and overpower her. "And I'm afraid I can't call for an ambulance because our phone hasn't been installed yet."

"We need the doctor," the woman insisted. "Where is he?"

"I'm sorry. My husband is...ill. We can't help you. There's another house about halfway down the hill, I'm sure there will be a phone there."

It occurred to Sarah then to wonder about the destination of the woman and her injured companion, since Cliff House stood alone at the pinnacle of a rocky peninsula.

"Nobody's home down the hill. They're probably summer people," the woman said. "Look, we've got to *do* something. My friend could be bleeding to death."

"Wait here," Sarah said. "I'll get my shoes and coat and drive you to the nearest phone."

Leaving the chain on the door, she ran back up the stairs. In her bedroom she opened the closet and pulled on her boots. Mark's father's old medical bag was on the closet shelf where she'd put it that afternoon and she grabbed it on her way out. As she recalled, there were still bandages, sterile pads, and tourniquets in the bag. She sped across the landing to Harriet's room.

The old woman lay on her back, her gossamer-soft hair a silver halo around her delicate features. Sarah patted her cheek gently. "Harriet, wake up."

Mark's grandmother twitched, then opened her eyes and stared at Sarah with the bewildered gaze of one lost in sleep.

"There's been an accident," Sarah said. "I'm going out. I'll leave your door open, just in case Emma wakes up. She probably won't but if she does, will you go to her? She might be frightened, waking up in a strange house."

"Accident," Harriet mumbled. "But...why are you going? Wake Mark up. He's the doctor."

"Harriet, Mark isn't here, remember?" Sarah said patiently. "He's in the hospital."

"Oh. Yes." Harriet's expression became anxious as she remembered the nature of Mark's malady. "But, Sarah, what can you do? You mustn't try to treat a patient. They could sue us."

"Just first aid, Harriet, I promise. But we've got to find a phone and get the paramedics out here."

Sarah ran back down the stairs, pulling on her jacket as she went. Quickly unhooking the chain, she opened the door only a crack and slid outside, almost colliding with her visitor. "The garage is over there," Sarah said quickly. "We can't get into it from the house."

They ran across the rain-slick driveway to the detached garage. Apparently Mark hadn't realized it would be inconvenient to have to cross a wide driveway to reach the garage. He'd been so entranced with the old house that nothing deterred him from buying it, not the isolation, the treacherously winding cliff road, nor the odd architecture.

Sarah raised the garage door and headed for the Jeep. Her visitor stopped to stare at the crumpled hood and smashed windshield of Mark's Mercedes. Sarah hadn't yet thought about having it repaired. She had too many other things to do and Mark certainly wouldn't be driving in the foreseeable future. She said, "Get in the Jeep."

Fastening her seat belt, Sarah worried about how well her recently acquired driving skills would hold up on the dark road in a howling gale. A New Yorker born and bred, she had never bothered to learn to drive until Mark insisted she take driving lessons before they moved to the West Coast, telling her that without a car she would be immobilized.

The headlight beams sliced through blackness filled with swirling diamonds of rain as she pulled out onto the gravel driveway. It was so damned dark up here. No streetlights, no neighbors. No town or village had sprung up around the ancient lighthouse that had predated Cliff House, probably because no other lights had been allowed to interfere with the warnings beamed out to passing ships. The cliff under the lighthouse had begun to erode and the lighthouse had been pulled down before the turn of the century. A local man who had fought the destruction of the landmark had bought the site and built a round three-story structure resembling a small lighthouse.

Sarah peered through the river of water her windshield wipers could barely keep at bay. "How far down the road is your car?"

"Not far. What's wrong with the doctor?"

"Wrong?"

"You said he was sick."

"Oh, yes. He . . . was injured. What did you say your name was?"

"I didn't. It's Mae. Mae Peterson. You're Mrs. Lasiter, right?"

"How did you know that? For that matter, how did you know a doctor had bought Cliff House?"

"It's my business to know, Mrs. Lasiter. I'm a Realtor."

"But it was a private sale—the house wasn't listed on the multiple listing board—" She broke off. "Is that your car?"

"It's not mine, but it's the car I was in."

The winding road widened into a lookout point and Sarah braked. Twenty feet from the lookout point the driver of a black Porsche had evidently missed the turn and rammed into the guardrail. The extent of the damage was difficult to see on the dark road, but both doors were wide open.

As Sarah pulled into the lookout area, the Jeep's headlights picked up the Nevada license plates on the Porsche. She set the hand brake and jumped out. The rain-driven wind took her breath away. Grabbing the medical bag, she ran to the Porsche.

There was no sign of anyone, injured or otherwise, anywhere near the car. Bewildered, Sarah tentatively ran her hand over the driver's seat. It was damp with rain but there was no telltale stickiness indicating blood.

Wheeling around, she saw that Mae Peterson was still sitting in the Jeep. Sarah yelled into the wind, "Where is he? Was he conscious when you left? For God's sake, get over here and help me find him. Bring the flashlight from the glove box."

Mae climbed slowly out of the Jeep and approached the Porsche. Sarah snatched the flashlight from her, sweeping the thin beam of light down the sheer cliff. One glance told her that if the injured man had plunged over the edge, there was nothing to break his fall. He would have crashed to the rocks below, where a savage winter surf sent towering plumes of white spray exploding into the cove.

Sarah turned away, breathless from the onslaught of the wind and stinging rain coming straight off the Pacific. She silently thanked God that Mark had not gone over the cliff at this spot. Still, there had been two accidents on the sparsely-traveled road in less than a week. It was nerve-racking.

Mae stood motionless beside the Porsche, watching her. Something in the woman's stance bothered Sarah and she moved away from the edge of the cliff.

"There was no injured man, was there?" she said angrily. "You were alone in the car."

"No! I *was* with a man. I didn't know him very well. He was knocked cold when we hit the guardrail. He must have come to and hitched a ride back to town."

How many cars came up a cliff road with only two houses on it, especially at midnight on a night like this?

"Get back into the Jeep," Sarah said grimly. "I'll drive you to town."

She drove slowly now, fearful of the hairpin bends. Mae Peterson sat silently beside her. They passed the other house, an A-frame cabin, which Mae had said was a summer residence. This was probably true, as it appeared to be dark, although at midnight that probably didn't mean anything. Sarah was relieved when they reached the Coast Highway and the lights of Emerald Cove shone through the curtain of rain.

"You can let me out at the gas station," Mae said.

"I'll drive you to the police station," Sarah answered. "There may be an injured man out there. You have to report the accident."

"I have to make a call before I talk to the police. Besides, I expect he's already reported the accident. Like I told you, I hardly knew him and it isn't my car."

"Yet you cared enough to walk all the way up to the top of the cliff and get me out of bed. You know, it wouldn't have been much farther for you to walk down to the highway."

"I didn't think. I was ... stunned, you know. Not thinking clearly. Besides, I knew a doctor had bought Cliff House."

"My husband is a psychiatrist, not a medical doctor."

"Psychiatrists have medical training."

A slow chill marked its way up Sarah's spine. She decided to stop at the first gas station and rid herself of this oddly disturbing woman. In an attempt to change the subject from Mark, she asked, "Do you live here in town? I noticed the Porsche had Nevada plates."

"I just moved here from Las Vegas."

"I thought you said you were in real estate here?"

"Not here. In Las Vegas."

"Then how—" Sarah bit back the questions. *How did you know we had bought Cliff House?* "There's a gas station. I'll drop you by the pay phone. Do you need change?"

"I've got a credit card."

Feeling glad to see the brightly lit service station, Sarah stopped the Jeep and waited for her passenger to leave. Mae Peterson turned to look at her then, a slow appraisal that made Sarah's skin crawl. In the well-lit parking area she saw now that the woman was older than she had at first assumed. The long blond hair and oversize black leather jacket had probably given the impression of youth. Now Sarah saw the fine lines around her eyes, which were an almost transparent gray. Probably mid to late thirties, Sarah decided, noting the arresting face with its pale, translucent complexion, high cheekbones and full lips.

Had it been minutes, or merely seconds, that the woman remained motionless, studying her with almost clinical intensity? What was she thinking? That Sarah's sleep-tossed brown hair badly needed styling, that there were fatigue circles under her deep blue eyes? The strain of the past twenty-four hours was no doubt written clearly on her face.

"I really need to get back to my family," Sarah said.

"*Your* family," Mae repeated, not moving.

"Yes. Are you sure you're all right? Sometimes shock sets in after an accident."

"I'm okay." Mae opened the door and stepped outside, hesitated a moment, still staring at Sarah, then slammed the door.

As she turned to walk away Sarah realized that the most significant aspect of the woman's appearance had at first escaped her. Mae Peterson was paler than a nun. That translucent complexion hadn't seen the sun in years. A difficult feat in Nevada.

Chapter Two

The storm had passed, leaving swept-clean skies of pale winter blue and a placid indigo ocean. Sunlight spilled into the kitchen through the floor-to-ceiling windows that formed a semicircle, defining the breakfast area. The ground floor of Cliff House consisted of the spacious kitchen, a pantry, and an entry hall of impressive proportions, into which the spiral staircase descended. The living areas were on the second floor and bedrooms on the third.

Sarah picked up Emma's untouched bowl of oatmeal. "Would you like some scrambled eggs, Emma?"

The little girl shook her honey-colored curls, her grave hazel eyes fixed accusingly on Sarah. "Want Daddy."

"I know, sweetie, but Daddy has to stay in the hospital until he's all better."

"When are you going to the hospital, Sarah?" Harriet asked as she came into the room.

"Right away, if you don't mind staying here. They're supposed to install the phone today."

Despite her interrupted sleep and the shock she'd received upon her arrival in California, Mark's grandmother looked surprisingly spry this morning. She was an elegant woman, tall and lean like her grandson, always carefully dressed and groomed. She had been unfailingly polite toward Sarah, but it was the common courtesy she might bestow on a stranger. Sarah wondered if the elderly lady was adopting a wait-and-see attitude toward her, in view of the defection of Mark's first wife.

Harriet poured herself a cup of coffee, frowning slightly at Emma's untouched cereal bowl. "Maybe you should take her with you to the hospital. You know, it's worse for a child to imagine than to actually see what's going on."

Sarah thought of the tubes and monitors keeping her husband alive, of the bandages and splints, and most of all, of his unnatural sleep. How could she explain a coma to a four-year-old? How could she explain that the doctors didn't know when, if ever, Mark would return to them? And if he did wake up, would he be the same man?

"Maybe you can go see Daddy soon. We'll see," Sarah said. *When the bruises begin to fade and some of the dressings are gone and oh, God, please, when he comes out of the coma.*

Harriet sat down next to the child and slipped her arm around her. "No monsters, honey. Just a lot of wind and rain. You'll like it here when you get used to it. It's hard for all of us to have to start over. But this is where Daddy wants to live."

Not for the first time, Sarah wondered about Mark's decision to uproot his daughter and grandmother. He had given up a successful psychiatric practice in Manhattan and a home on Long Island. Shortly before their wedding, to Sarah's astonishment, he'd abruptly asked how she felt about moving to a remote area of Northern California and helping him write the book he'd been planning for years.

Sarah had looked forward to the move. Mark's friends had not exactly welcomed her into their closed circle. Eminent psychiatrists were not supposed to marry their office managers, especially not when they were former patients as well. Besides, she loved being with Mark and the prospect of helping him prepare his manuscript had appealed to her.

Then, too, there was Emma, who was such a lost little soul, so quiet and withdrawn. No one talked about how her mother had abandoned her, when Emma was only eighteen months old, and Sarah wanted so much to heal the hurt she knew both Emma and Mark felt.

Sarah put her dishes in the sink and turned to Harriet. "We have eggs and oatmeal. I'll pick up some groceries while I'm in town."

"Don't worry about me. I'll fix myself something. Why don't you get started, so you'll be back for lunch?"

The doorbell rang and Sarah said, "Oh, good, that will be the telephone company. I'll let them in."

But there was no sign of a telephone company truck parked outside, or any other vehicle, and the man standing on her doorstep carried no tools. He appeared to be in his midthirties. Tousled sandy hair and twinkling amber eyes were set in a weathered face that spoke of long hours outdoors. Broad shoulders strained a faded denim jacket and he wore sturdy boots of the type construction workers favored. He carried a clay pot holding a gray-green cactus from which sprouted graceful lavender-colored flowers as beautiful as any orchid.

"Hi, I'm your neighbor down the hill. Ben Travis. Just got back today and heard you'd moved in. Stopped by to introduce myself and welcome you to our hill."

"I'm so glad we have a neighbor. We thought you were only here during the summer."

"No, I'm year-round. But I take business trips sometimes."

He held out the potted cactus and Sarah took it from him. "Oh . . . thank you. It's lovely."

"And indestructible," he assured her with a grin that transformed his weathered face. "You won't be able to kill it no matter how hard you try. If you do want to kill it, we'll have to hire a hit man."

Sarah smiled politely. "I'd invite you in, but I was just getting ready to leave. My husband is in the hospital."

"I'm sorry. Nothing serious, I hope? Well, I guess that's a stupid question, since he's in the hospital."

"He was in an accident a couple of days ago. Driving up here, as a matter of fact. I was still back East, getting ready to move."

Ben Travis nodded sympathetically. "Some bad bends on this road for the unwary."

"Speaking of which, have they removed the Porsche yet?"

He looked puzzled. "Porsche?"

"There was another accident last night about midnight. A Porsche missed the turn and smashed into the guardrail, just south of the lookout point."

"I didn't notice any damage to the rail when I drove up and there's no sign of a car. I doubt that a tow truck driver would come up here in the dark, so it couldn't have been seriously damaged. Well, I'd better let you go see your husband."

He turned to leave and Sarah said, "I'll look forward to meeting your wife. Perhaps we can get together as soon as we're settled in?"

Glancing back over his shoulder, Ben's expression was sadly resigned. "Sorry, I'm a widower."

"Any children?" Sarah asked, then realizing she sounded too eager, explained, "We have a four-year-old daughter. I was hoping there might be another child up here for her to play with."

He shook his head. "Just me."

She watched as he walked down the driveway, moving with the easy stride of one long-accustomed to the steep terrain. He had just turned onto the road when a black Mercedes that could have been the twin of Mark's car before the accident turned into the driveway.

It certainly wouldn't be the phone company, Sarah thought. She remained at the door until the car reached the house. Her stomach lurched as she saw who was at the wheel. Mae Peterson. Quickly Sarah put the cactus down on the porch, and walked out onto the driveway to meet her visitor.

This morning the mysterious Ms. Peterson wore a conservative black suit and her long blond hair was swept up into a French braid. Her car also had Nevada plates. She carried a pink bakery box.

"Good morning," Sarah said uncertainly.

"Hi, how are you?" Mae's smile didn't reach her pale eyes. "I came by to thank you for the ride last night and to apologize for getting you out of bed. I didn't know about your husband. I wouldn't have bothered you if I had. Pretty tough on you, being stuck up here with a kid and an old lady and the doctor in a coma. What's the prognosis?"

"The doctors are hopeful," Sarah replied uneasily.

"I hear he lost control of the car not far from where we had our accident last night."

"Yes. Have you spoken to your friend yet? Is he all right?"

The transparent eyes blinked. "My friend?"

"The owner of the Porsche. I hear it's already been removed."

"Uh-huh. He's fine. I guess I panicked last night. My friend must've come to, got a ride to town and brought a tow truck up right away."

"I'm surprised he was able to find one in the middle of the night."

Mae shrugged. "Maybe the Porsche was drivable." She held out the pink box. "Brought you a coffee cake to show my gratitude."

"Thank you, but that really wasn't necessary."

"Maybe we could have a cup of coffee and visit for a while? I'm new in town, just like you. It's always hard to make friends in a strange place, isn't it?"

"Well…you see, I was just leaving for the hospital. Some other time, perhaps?" Sarah felt ungracious, but there was something vaguely threatening about this woman.

"Sure, I understand," Mae said easily. "Maybe grandma and the little girl would like to share the cake with me?"

"No," Sarah said sharply. "I mean, they're not up yet." The fact that Mae Peterson had asked enough questions about them to learn of Mark's coma and the presence of Emma and Harriet was unsettling.

Mae glanced over her shoulder toward the house, as if doubting this, then raised a pale blond eyebrow questioningly. "I really must ask you to excuse me now," Sara said. "We're just not set up for visitors yet."

For a long moment they stood staring at each other in some sort of unspoken challenge, then Mae shoved the bakery box into Sarah's hands and walked back to her car.

Sarah went back into the house, breathing unevenly, more shaken by the encounter than she thought was warranted. Perhaps it was simply the crush of recent events and being left in charge of this isolated house. The round house had narrow windows on either side of the frosted-glass front door and Harriet was standing beside one of them, staring at the retreating Mercedes. She gripped the window frame as if to support herself. Her face was ashen.

"What's wrong?" Sarah asked. "Do you know that woman?"

Harriet shook her head, but Sarah could see she was trembling.

"Are you sure? Harriet, you're shaking like a leaf."

"I thought she was driving Mark's car, that's all. But then I remembered, his is all banged up from the accident."

Sarah wasn't convinced. The older woman rarely showed distress, or any other emotion resembling fear. The door was slightly ajar and she wondered if Harriet had overheard their conversation and been bothered by it. Perhaps, like herself, she felt there was something strange about Mae Peterson.

A telephone truck arrived then, and Sarah collected her bag and jacket and headed for the hospital.

MARK AND AN ELDERLY MAN who had suffered a massive heart attack were the only patients in the intensive care unit of the small seaside hospital. Sarah sat beside her comatose husband, holding his unbandaged hand, speaking in a low voice.

"Well, we're moved in. There was a tremendous storm last night. It was weird, being up at the top of the cliff with the wind and rain lashing all the uncurtained windows. A bit like being in a goldfish bowl. Yet in a way, all the noise of the gale was better than the silence when it was over. I suppose I miss the night noise of New York. I've really got to do something about drapes or shutters or something. Especially for Emma's room. She misses you dreadfully, of course. Harriet seems to be taking it all in stride."

Mark's eyes remained closed, his body motionless. Sarah stared at him, feeling all her doubts well up again. What if he never came out of the coma? People had lived for years in such states.

The future loomed vague and uncertain. Sarah felt overwhelmed by the enormity of the responsibility Mark had, unwittingly, thrust upon her. But even more than the stress of being forced to cope without him, she was experiencing a sinking sense of dismay that she had married a stranger. How much did she know about Mark Lasiter, really? She had gone from patient to office manager to wife with very little transition time or preparation.

During these last frantic forty-eight hours since she had arrived in California to find him in a coma, she'd had to find her way to a house she had never seen before while trying to keep Emma and Harriet calm. She'd put them in a motel the first night and remained at the hospital with her husband. But the confinement of the motel added to their anxiety, so Sarah decided to move into the house. Seeing the location, she'd understood Mark's insistence that she learn to drive and was glad to find the Jeep waiting in the garage. She had expected a quiet and serene location, but not near-total isolation.

Oh, Mark, she thought, *why did you insist on coming out here alone? Why didn't we stay together? You could just as easily have waited for us. Maybe you wouldn't have fallen asleep at the wheel, or missed the turn, or whatever happened to cause the accident, if I'd been with you. Besides, I'm not sure Cliff House would have been my first choice.*

As she waited for the nurse to finish her ministrations, Sarah found herself reexamining the events of the scant three months that had preceded her wedding.

She supposed she had been dazzled by the brilliant psychiatrist who was not only dedicated to helping patients deal with their problems, but who also cared for an elderly grandmother and a four-year-old daughter.

Mark had helped Sarah overcome paralyzing depression after her parents and fiancé were killed in a hotel fire. She had left the floor where the fire had started only minutes before it exploded in flames. She had been forcedly restrained from going back. Afterward her grief had been mixed with guilt that she had survived while the three people she loved most in the world had not. The fire had taken their lives on what was to have been Sarah's wedding day. Months had passed before she sought help.

When she began to come out of her depression and talk about going back to work, Mark had offered her a job in his office. At first she had been a little in awe of him. Certainly, she was grateful to have an engrossing job as well as a sympathetic employer. Mark was always so much in charge, never showing hesitancy or doubt, that she had been surprised and touched, when those traits suddenly surfaced.

One morning he abruptly asked her to have lunch with him, saying there were things he wanted to discuss that could not be brought up at the office. They went to a small Italian place, called Pasquale's Ristorante, with checkered tablecloths and candles in Chianti bottles. They sat in a secluded corner and for the first time Mark revealed a vulnerable, hurting side that she had not suspected existed.

"I'm a psychiatrist," he'd said, "yet I don't know whether I'm handling Emma correctly. I sent her to a colleague for a while, but she became even more withdrawn, so I stopped the therapy. She was simply too young to understand why she doesn't have a mother like other children. I suppose neither of us has ever really dealt with the loss of her mother." He twisted the stem of his wineglass, gazing into some distant memory that brought a tortured veil down over his eyes.

Sarah had waited silently, unsure what to say.

Abruptly his mood changed, becoming brisk and businesslike again. "Sarah, you're a sensible young woman who seems to deal with people and situations well. My daughter is cared for by my grandmother, who's getting up in years. I have a housekeeper, too, but English isn't her first language. Now what I'm going to ask is certainly not part of your job description, but... well, would you accompany Emma and me to the zoo this Saturday?"

The request had come out of left field, but she said yes. She had been drawn to Emma immediately. The little girl had her father's large, grave eyes and a childish version of his dignity. Emma had spent most of her life with an elderly woman and was far too quiet and well behaved. She didn't seem to know how to play, or laugh, and heaven forbid she should disobey an adult. Often for no apparent reason, she would start to cry softly, then disappear into herself, shutting out the world.

Sarah soon found herself spending almost all her free time with Mark and Emma, although never at his home. She did meet his grandmother on the occasion of Emma's fourth birthday. Harriet had been polite but distant.

Mark was different away from the office, frequently witty and lighthearted, treating her as a respected friend. They never spent any time alone, yet Sarah knew she was getting far too comfortable with their arrangement. He and Emma were becoming the entire focus of her life and Sarah worried that she was setting herself up for heartbreak.

About a month after her trip to the zoo with Mark and Emma, she noticed he began to show signs of strain, almost agitation. He forgot appointments, misplaced files and seemed distracted and jumpy. Sarah put it down to the stress of dealing with some particularly difficult patients.

Then one evening he asked her to have dinner with him—alone. They went to the same small, out-of-the way Italian restaurant where they'd had lunch. But this time, Mark unexpectedly reached across the table and captured her hand in his. "What do you want out of life, Sarah? Do you have a long-term goal?"

She wondered how she could give him an honest answer. To tell her employer that making appointments and feeding data into a computer was not her lifelong ambition seemed counterproductive. But to confide in a dear friend that she longed for a home and children of her own and a quiet place to write and illustrate children's stories . . . After a moment she told him the truth and the expression of wonder on his face surely was not feigned.

"Sarah, this is the most incredible coincidence," he'd said. "You see, I've been working on a book for years now—I've never had enough time to finish it—and lately I've been thinking of giving up my practice to write full-time."

"Is it a book about psychiatry?" she'd asked.

"Well, yes and no. It's a novel, actually. But based on one of my more…intriguing cases. And, of course, therein lies the problem. I have to tread a fine line between truth and fiction, being careful not to break the rules of confidentiality between doctor and patient. Frankly, I could use an impartial critic, not to mention someone conversant with word processors to put the whole thing down on paper."

He was about to ask her to assist him with his book, Sarah thought, and she felt unaccountably disappointed but was unsure why. She'd said, "Your patients are going to miss you. I don't suppose you could continue your

practice and still get your book finished if you had someone to help?''

"I know of another psychiatrist who's eager to take over
my practice. Money won't be a problem. My father made
some wise investments and left Nana and me healthy trust
funds."

There was a long pause, as if he were carefully weighing
his words, then he said, "Some years ago I took Emma on
a vacation to the West Coast. After we did Disneyland, the
Wild Animal Park and Sea World, I rented a car and we
drove up the coast to Big Sur and then further north to
Mendocino."

His gaze seemed to seek that distant place, looking not
so much at Sarah, as beyond her. When he spoke again his
voice was so low he seemed to be thinking aloud. "Such
wild, beautiful country. Rugged, lonely, yet so serene."

Acutely aware of his hand enclosing hers, Sarah waited.
All at once, Mark seemed to snap back from wherever his
memory had taken him to the present and to her. "Sarah,
these past weeks I've been so grateful for the way you've
taken Emma to your heart. The relationship between you
is . . . well, let's just say you've done more for my daughter
in days than her therapist accomplished in months."

"Emma is a wonderful little girl. Too sad and serious for
her age, but she really seems to be coming out of her shell,
doesn't she?''

"Yes, indeed. Where did you ever learn so much about
children?''

Sarah had laughed. "We lived next door to a family of
seven kids—three of them toddlers when they first moved
in. I spent most of my teens baby-sitting. Besides, I love
children."

"The neighbors might have given you experience, but I
believe you're one of those people blessed with a rare em-

pathy for children. Too many of us forget what it's like to be little and helpless, subject to the whims and rages of creatures three or four times our size.''

Later, she would wonder if that was the moment she fell in love with Mark.

He went on, ''But you know, Sarah, between taking Emma on outings and working together, we're always surrounded by people. You and I have never been able to move into the kind of relationship I for one would like to have. Now I must ask you, could you ever see me as more than Emma's father? Could you spend your days with me if I were more than your employer?''

''Dr. Lasiter...I—''

''Mark. Please call me Mark.''

''Mark, I admire you tremendously. I never dared consider... She fumbled for words. Distant warning voices were striving to be heard. *It's too soon! You don't know each other! Stop this before it goes any further. You need time!*

He drew her to her feet. ''Come on, let's go home. I have a feeling we're going to be up all night, talking about the future.''

For the first time, he took her to his home on Long Island. She saw the For Sale sign on the front lawn, but he made no comment. Both Emma and Harriet had retired for the night and Mark lit a fire in the living room and went into the kitchen to open a bottle of wine.

She was aware of a pleasing mix of antique and contemporary furniture, several Dalis and what appeared to be an authentic Cezanne on the walls, and a forest of plants. But there was a curiously impersonal feeling to the room that she couldn't quite define. Perhaps she had been expecting photographs or mementos of some sort, hinting that his wife had once lived here.

Mark returned with their wine and immediately began to speak in a way that suggested he had rehearsed what he was about to say.

"There's been no one in my life since my wife left. I never wanted to feel that kind of pain again. Then I watched you reach out to Emma, despite your own pain and loss, and day by day I saw you calmly dealing with the most trying people, overcoming your own grief by being more concerned with the problems of others."

"Oh, Mark," Sarah murmured, "I'm awed by how kind and compassionate you are. You've never once even hinted about the tragedy of your wife, nor allowed it to affect your work. You've never acted sorry for yourself."

He slipped his arm around her shoulders. "I think I began to live again the day you walked into my life, although I didn't know it then. You'll never know how difficult it is for me to work beside you every day and not tell you how I feel about you."

His hand cupped her face and the next moment they were kissing, tentatively at first, then with rising passion.

That night, he asked her to marry him. Almost surprising herself, Sarah had said yes. If she had felt any qualms about becoming Mrs. Mark Lasiter, there had simply been no time to examine them in their headlong dash into matrimony.

How could she had foreseen how quickly her husband would begin to withdraw into himself? There would be nights when she would awaken and he would not be at her side. She would find him sitting alone in the dark and he offered no explanation. She learned quickly to respect his need for solitude and to hide from him the fact that she had begun to feel lonely in a way she did not dare to define.

Her doubts about her marriage had begun even before Mark abruptly announced he was leaving, alone, and would be in touch with her when he found a place to live. He had not told her where, on four hundred miles of California coastline, he was going, and when a few days later he did call, she had the distinct feeling that his professed enthusiasm about her bringing Emma and Harriet to join him at Cliff House was forced.

Now, staring at her husband's prone figure in the hospital bed, she tried to assure herself that there was an explanation for his strange behavior.

Chapter Three

"Daddy, Daddy, there's a monster!"

Emma's terrified screams awoke Sarah. She stumbled out of bed and raced to the child's room.

Switching on the bedside lamp. Sarah tried to gather the little girl into her arms, but Emma was rigid with fear and resisted.

"Emma, baby, it's all right, it was just a bad dream."

The child fought her. "Want my Daddy!"

"Sweetie, he's in the hospital. He isn't here, remember? But Nana and I are here and we'll take care of you. Look, there's no monster."

Wide-eyed with fear, Emma pointed to the French doors that opened to a wooden balcony. "He was out there. I saw him. He was coming to get me."

Sarah walked over to the French doors and looked out. "No monsters out there, sweetie."

"He's hiding now."

"Then I'll go outside and look for him. You wait there in bed, okay?"

A chill breeze took Sarah's breath away as she stepped out onto the balcony. The ocean was a vast, undulating silver cloak wrapped from horizon to rocky shoreline. Shivering in her cotton nightgown, Sarah walked from one end of the balcony to the other, passing the French doors that opened to the master bedroom.

All of the rooms on the ocean side of the house opened onto balconies. There were two balconies and a ground floor deck, one above the other, and all were connected by flights of wooden steps. When Mark had called her to say he had found their dream house, he'd said the balconies had been one of the features that charmed him. But his grandmother had elected to take a room on the other side of the house, without a balcony.

"No monsters, nothing out there, honey. Just a few shadows. How about I get you some warm milk and read you a story?"

THE WINDING ROAD WAS becoming more familiar to her, Sarah told herself without much conviction as she drove down the hill on her way to town the following morning.

Ben Travis was working on the low stone wall enclosing his front yard, replacing a section that had evidently crumbled. She was struck by the ease with which he handled the heavy rocks and couldn't help but notice that the motion of his powerful shoulders and arms could almost be described as graceful. It was, she thought, a strange adjective to pop into her mind in view of his rugged build and craggy features.

He waved her to a stop. She pulled over reluctantly, telling herself she had a lot to do after visiting Mark at the hospital, but aware that her reluctance owed more to her disquieting interest in her new neighbor.

"Morning, Mrs. Lasiter, you getting all settled in?"

"Yes, thank you." She didn't turn off the engine.

"Just wanted to say that if you need a handyman while your husband's laid up, don't hesitate to call me. I can pretty well turn my hand to anything."

"That's very kind of you. Is that your business?"

He smiled. "I guess you might say so. I also do a little painting and sculpting."

Realization dawned then. She clapped her hand to her mouth in embarrassment. "*Travis.* Of course! I didn't connect the name—how stupid of me. I saw some of your work in the hospital. Those wonderful marine life paintings. Someone said you have several of them on exhibition in the gallery in town. I asked because I'll need something to put on the walls of a round house. Choosing pictures—furniture, too—will be a problem when there isn't a flat area anywhere."

"Maybe I could help? I'd be glad to come and take a look. Round rooms must be a real challenge to decorate. My wife was an interior designer, and I picked up a few hints from her."

Sarah murmured noncommittally, knowing Harriet would be horrified if she invited a single man to visit during Mark's absence.

"You hear anything further about the Porsche you saw crashed into the guardrail the other night?" Ben asked.

"As a matter of fact, the passenger—a woman named Mae Peterson—called on me. She seemed to blow off the whole thing. When I asked she said her friend must have come to and driven away. I don't suppose you know anything about her, do you? She's new in town, a real estate broker from Nevada. I assume she's going into business in Emerald Cove."

He shook his head. "Never heard of her." He looked at Sarah questioningly. "But I did wonder why somebody in a car accident would walk *up* the hill instead of down. If she's new in town, how did she even know there was a house up there? You can't see it from where the car crashed."

"She not only knew it was there, she also knew it had been bought by a doctor. I've been wondering about that, too."

"Mae Peterson, you say? I'll ask around town and see what I can find out."

"Oh, that's not necessary. She probably won't be back. Well, I'd really better get going."

Sarah pulled onto the road again. Her rearview mirror told her that Ben Travis watched until she was out of sight.

HOLDING HER HUSBAND'S limp hand, Sarah said, "I dreamed about Cape Cod last night. That quaint old inn where we spent our honeymoon. I guess the sound of the sea here reminded me."

A nurse appeared and began to change IV bottles and Sarah lapsed into silence, memory taking her back to disturbing incidents on their brief honeymoon. She had come upon her husband speaking in furtive whispers on the phone, and he'd hung up as soon as he'd seen her.

When they returned to Manhattan, Mark suggested she stay in her apartment rather than move into the Long Island house for what would only be a temporary stay. He also asked that she take Emma and Harriet, so that they would be spared the upheaval of packing and vacating the only home the child had ever known. It had been a tight fit to find room for them in Sarah's tiny apartment.

Later, after she left the Emerald Cove hospital and was driving back to Cliff House, Sarah found herself thinking of those posthoneymoon days again. She had been left virtually in charge of the office and had seen very little of Mark. When she did, he seemed to be jumpy and distracted once more. She had put it down to the stress of closing the sale of his house and natural misgivings about changing his life-style.

When Mark called to say he had decided to buy Cliff House Sarah had asked if the furniture from Long Island would fit and he'd answered, almost offhandedly, "I'm not shipping the furniture. Let's make a completely new start in California. You can furnish Cliff House to your taste. I'll just arrange to ship our personal stuff."

At the time it seemed like a rare gift, being given the opportunity to furnish her very own house. Mark had purchased only the essentials in the week he'd spent alone, and now she wondered when she would be able to find time to fill those empty round walls. She had to spend as much time with Mark as possible, hoping against hope the sound of her voice could break through that impenetrable fog that had him in its grip, yet Emma needed her, too. The house would have to wait.

Arriving at Cliff House again, she found several packing cases standing in the entry hall. Their personal belongings had evidently arrived.

"Hi, I'm home," she called.

"We're up here in Emma's room," Harriet's muffled voice responded.

Sarah ran up the spiral staircase, but stopped short at the doorway to Emma's room. The furniture was gone.

Turning away, she crossed the circular landing to the bedrooms on the inland side of the house, one of which was Harriet's. She saw at once that Emma's bed and chest of drawers had been moved into the room next door to Harriet's. Emma and her great-grandmother were aligning newly arrived stuffed animals along a window seat.

"We decided Emma would be happier in this room," Harriet said, a faint note of disapproval in her tone, as if Sarah should have realized this from the first. "There's no balcony for monsters to climb up. Besides, I believe the sound of the surf bothered her in the other room. I'll be right next door and I'll hear her if she wakes up in the night."

"I heard her last night," Sarah said defensively. "I put her next to the master bedroom not only because it's a larger room with an ocean view, but also so you wouldn't be disturbed."

Harriet ignored the remark and picked up a rather battered teddy bear. "Oh, look, Emmie, here's Mr. Buttons." She said to Sarah, "We lost him amid the new arrivals. Thank goodness we found him."

Mr. Buttons was Emma's constant companion. He'd lost his eyes years ago and someone had sewn large pearl buttons in their place.

"How did you ever manage to dismantle the bed and move it over here, Harriet?"

"Our neighbor did it," Harriet replied.

"What? Who?"

"Ben, Ben Travis. He lives down the hill. Such a nice man. He's an artist."

"He was here, while I was gone? And you let him in?"

Harriet straightened up. "Do I need your permission to invite someone into this house?"

"No, of course not. It's just that . . . well, we don't know anything about Ben Travis. And I know he saw me leaving earlier, so he made a point of coming while I was away. That bothers me."

"He came to leave a message for you. He said as you were driving down the hill he noticed that the rear wheel of the Jeep seemed to be wobbling. He tried to call the hospital to warn you, but you weren't there." The old lady's tone was now accusing.

"I decided to buy some material for curtains before I visited Mark," Sarah said, feeling more defensive than ever.

"Yes, well, Ben said he was going into town, and he wanted me to tell you not to drive the Jeep again until he checks the wheel. He saw that the packing cases had arrived and asked if he could move them for me. I had him carry Emma's things up here and told him we were moving her into the other room, so he offered to move her furniture, too."

Sarah looked down at Emma. "If this is the room you want, sweetie, it's fine by me. I'll make you some curtains for the window. In fact I bought so much material for the French doors in the other room, there'll be enough to make a matching bedspread."

Emma clutched Mr. Buttons tightly. She nodded gravely.

"Okay, I'll fix lunch. Give me ten minutes."

Neither Harriet nor Emma came down for lunch, despite Sarah's call upstairs that it was ready. She fixed a fresh pot of coffee, then took a tray of sandwiches and milk up to them.

She took her own sandwich into the hall, and began to unpack the boxes. The first contained books. She took them to the built-in bookcases in the second floor room. Mark had laughingly dubbed his new study "the captain's mess" because it contained a collection of maritime objects and fishing tackle left behind by the previous owner.

Nibbling her sandwich, Sarah stood in the room, trying to imagine Mark seated at a desk. She conjured images of him checking the time on the ship's brass clock, glancing at the bottled galleon, and idly playing with the antique sextant as he planned the next segment of his book. But suddenly Mark faded from the picture, replaced by the bandage-swathed stranger in the hospital. Suppressing a qualm, she went back to the unpacking.

At the bottom of the book box were several manila envelopes and file folders secured with rubber bands. She removed them and stacked them on the floor. As she did so, one of the rubber bands broke and the file spilled its contents onto the floor.

Picking up the papers, she was about to shove them back into the file when she saw the word *kill*.

Her heart pounding, she read the typewritten page, which contained a single paragraph.

Damn you to hell, Mark Lasiter,
   You cold, unfeeling bastard! You're not getting away with this. You'd better sleep with one eye open.
   I haven't decided yet which of you to kill first.

Chapter Four

There was no address or signature on the letter, but there was a date that resonated in Sarah's mind. It was the date of her wedding to Mark.

Quickly turning to the rest of the file, she found several handwritten pages and recognized Mark's sprawling script. She read rapidly.

Prologue
The letter arrived on Matt Layton's wedding day. No time to get to the office and pull the files, but he was pretty sure the threat had come from one or two clients. Both of whom were potentially dangerous.

Sarah sighed in relief. These were the notes for Mark's novel. His protagonist was Matt Layton, which sounded a little too close to Mark Lasiter for comfort, but she supposed a first-time novelist would be prone to use his own alter-ego as his main character.

She turned to the typewritten page again. Why had he used his real name there? And why wasn't the letter included in the prologue? He'd used their real wedding date, which was curious. Her heart started to beat more rapidly.

Was it possible the letter was a real threat, sent to him on their wedding day?

Turning back to the handwritten manuscript, she saw that the second paragraph had been crossed out, then Mark had written: *But is this the prologue or the epilogue? Maybe I should go back and tell it chronologically?*

"What are you doing?" Harriet's shrill question caused Sarah to jump.

Harriet was coming down the stairs at a speed that seemed perilous considering her age. "Are you going through Mark's papers?"

Sarah, who was on her knees, sat back on her haunches and closed the file. "I'm unpacking, Harriet. We can't just leave these boxes lying here."

"You were reading Mark's private papers," Harriet accused.

"As a matter of fact," Sarah answered carefully, "what I was looking at are the notes for Mark's book. I thought you knew I was going to be working on it with him."

Harriet's lips compressed into a disapproving line and she went back upstairs. Sarah stared after her. What did Harriet think she was looking for? Sarah had naturally been curious about Mark's first wife but she'd never asked Harriet about her after Mark's terse explanation, "Tamara left us. I destroyed every trace of her and we never speak her name."

The doorbell rang and Sarah stood up. Through the frosted-glass panel she recognized the tousled hair and broad shoulders of Ben Travis. Opening the door, she saw he was carrying a toolbox. "Saw you driving up the hill a while ago. Figured you'd be eating lunch so I didn't chase you home. But I didn't want you to drive the Jeep again until I check that right rear wheel."

"Harriet told me about it. I was going to stop off at a garage in town. I really don't want to impose—"

"It will only take a minute. Indulge me, okay? This road is too tricky to risk losing a wheel."

Given what had happened to Mark, Ben Travis had a point. Sarah decided to let him look at the Jeep, which was in the driveway, while she continued to unpack. Taking as many files and envelopes as she could carry, she went up to her bedroom and put them on a shelf at the back of the closet. She stood in the closet for a moment, still shaken by the possible death threat against her husband.

Several questions hammered at her brain. She had never seen Mark use a typewriter; in fact she hadn't been aware he owned one. At the office she had worked on a computer. Even if Mark did own a typewriter, why did he type only the threatening letter and not the prologue or notes? Was the use of his own name in the threat merely a slip?

She recalled that Mark had told her his novel was based on an actual case, but she had assumed it was from long ago. It seemed far too risky to fictionalize current clients, yet the date of the death threat had been only scant weeks ago.

The doorbell rang again and she ran downstairs.

Ben Travis still had a wrench in his hand. His expression was grim. "Somebody loosened the lug nuts on that rear wheel, Mrs. Lasiter. You're lucky I spotted it wobbling. If you'd lost a wheel on this road..."

"Come in," Sarah said. "I think I need to sit down."

He followed her into the kitchen, laid the wrench down and washed his hands in the sink.

Sarah sat down at the kitchen table. "Please don't say anything about this in front of my husband's daughter or grandmother."

He reached for a towel to dry his hands. "I saw your husband's car in the garage. Did anybody check it over after his accident?"

Maybe someone should have. The chilling thought occurred to Sarah. But surely, any officers present the night of Mark's accident would have noticed evidence of foul play. She shook her head. "I keep meaning to call the insurance company, but I just haven't had time yet. I've had so much to do."

Ben poured two cups of coffee and brought them to the table. "Anybody have a grudge against you or your husband?"

"We don't know anybody here. We're both New Yorkers."

"Well, we'd better not jump to conclusions. Maybe your lug nuts just wore loose."

To her dismay, Sarah realized she was trembling. "But the Jeep is new, and so was Mark's Mercedes."

"Good thing you weren't in the car with him."

There was something reassuring about Ben's presence and Sarah felt an acute need to talk to somebody other than Harriet about the accident. "Mark came out ahead of us to find a house and buy the cars," she began. "The accident happened in the evening, right before we arrived. The car went over the cliff but it didn't crash onto the beach below. It wedged into those pines south of the lookout point."

"He was lucky somebody saw the accident. I was in San Francisco, you hadn't arrived yet, and nobody else drives up here."

"A highway patrolman saw it happen and radioed for an ambulance," Sarah said. "As soon as we arrived, I went to the hospital. The patrolman gave me the name of a tow truck company. I called and told them to bring the car here. I didn't know what else to do. The officer said it was a one-car accident. Mark had evidently either fallen asleep at the wheel or taken a turn too fast and gone into a skid. He was lucky he went over the edge where he did. It's the only place where there were pines to break the fall.''

''There was a police report?''

Sarah was beginning to feel embarrassed. ''Ben, I realize I should have asked more questions, and I probably should have noticed that the wheel of the Jeep was wobbling, but you have to understand, I've been under a lot of stress. Besides, I'm a New Yorker. I couldn't even drive a car a couple of months ago. I had to take a crash course—''

He raised an eyebrow.

''No pun intended,'' Sarah muttered.

''I'm sorry, I didn't mean to interrogate you. Look, if you'll give me your car keys I'll take the Jeep for a spin and check to be sure everything else is all right.''

Sarah got up to look for her handbag. Handing him the keys she asked, ''Why are you doing this for me? We're strangers.''

He shrugged. ''We're neighbors. Besides, I'd hope if I was faced with the situation you're in, somebody would lend me a hand.''

Sarah felt some of her tension ease. ''Harriet was right,'' she said softly.

''How's that?''

''She said you were a nice man.''

Ben's eyebrows arched quizzically. ''Did she tell you what I said about you?''

''No, she didn't.''

''I told her that the two qualities I admire most are guts and loyalty and that you have plenty of both. I was thinking, but didn't say, that most pretty women are too self-absorbed to give much thought to anything other than their own good looks, and that her grandson was lucky to find you.''

A THICK FOG had crept silently into the bay, covering Cliff House in a clammy gray cloudlike shroud. Sarah felt isolated, detached, a prisoner in this remote tower. After Harriet and Emma went to bed, she made a pot of tea and took it upstairs, pausing on the landing to listen. There was no sound from the bedrooms. She tried not to recall the comforting presence of Ben Travis. Even if he was off-limits, it was good to know he was close by.

She went into her room and retrieved Mark's files from the closet shelf. A quick check revealed that only one file folder contained notes for his book. The others were previous years' income tax statements and various investment portfolios. She was about to set these aside when when she noticed a folder marked Safety Deposit Box.

Inside, she found Emma's birth certificate, passports for Mark and Harriet, two insurance policies made out to Harriet in trust for Emma, and the deed to a house. For long panicked moments, Sarah looked at the Long Island parcel numbers on the deed. Was this the deed to the house Mark had supposedly just sold? If the house was sold, why would he still have the deed?

She looked for, but could not find, a divorce decree.

Picking up the manuscript folder again, she flipped past the death threat letter and began to read.

The notes were fragmented, disjointed, but several times it seemed Mark had attempted to place his alter ego, Matt Layton, in action. Sarah found herself ignoring the character sketches and psychological theories and looking for a fictional scene. A page marked Chapter One caught her attention.

Matt Layton regarded the woman sitting in the leather wing chair opposite him with what he hoped was professional interest but he had the uncomfortable feeling that his attraction might be obvious.

But even a psychiatrist had a right to be awestruck by his first sight of Selma Johnson. Take Marilyn Monroe's body and top it with a young Elizabeth Taylor's face. (no, work on description, too clichéd, need to capture that elusive magnetic quality of hers that went beyond beauty.)

At this point Mark had evidently decided to change to first person.

How can I describe my first meeting with Selma Johnson? It was somewhere between that feeling I had when I somersaulted over my skis and landed flat on my back with all the wind knocked out of me, and the struck-dumb homage I felt the first time I heard a symphony orchestra play Mozart.

Outside the wooden balcony creaked and Sarah looked up, half expecting the mesmerizing Selma to appear. But there was only that gray blanket of fog pressing against the glass of French doors and windows. Probably the expansion of the balcony wood in the dampness had caused the sound.

During the months Sarah had worked with Mark she recalled no such hauntingly beautiful patient as the one he had described. It was both revealing and dismaying to read his description of his fantasy woman. Sarah couldn't help comparing her own attributes. Her slender figure was certainly not voluptuous like Monroe's, nor did she consider herself a raving beauty, but she had a good complexion. Her eyes were her best feature, deep blue and framed by charcoal lashes and high arching brows. Her light brown hair, although thick and luxurious, had a mind of its own.

Mark's allusions to film stars of a previous era also reminded Sarah of the difference in their ages, and she wondered idly how old the luscious Selma would be now.

Sarah looked down at the manuscript again. Apparently Mark had made several false starts, switching back and forth between first and third person. Several pages appeared to be missing. Then she came across a page numbered eleven.

Selma brought Bryce with her today. I was surprised. I'd begun to think he was a figment of her imagination. I'd even considered he might be the other half of her dual state of mind. That duality exists, I'm convinced, although I've found not a shred of evidence that any of the events she's described actually occurred. Still, I'd wondered whether Bryce could be the Mr. Hyde to her Dr. Jekyll. Perhaps she had even, in a state of fugue, become the avenging Bryce, but had managed to conceal the evidence of his evil deeds. That possibility had troubled me from the time she first told her horrifying story.

Yet here he was, large as life and at least as ugly, glaring at me. He demanded to know how long my treatment was going to last, why I hadn't prescribed Prozac or Zanax like her previous shrink and how I expected to curb her simply by listening to her tell her wild stories.

Interesting choice of words. Curb her.

He's a big bruiser, with the battered face of a boxer and biceps like King Kong. (No, re-write that).

Attached to the next page was a note written on a small scrap of paper.

Isn't it normal to suppress—or integrate—our dark side? Maybe we're only truly stable when we allow our dark side to live within us separate but less than equal.

Sarah rubbed her eyes, which were half-closed with exhaustion. Mark's handwriting was difficult to decipher and the words were blurring.

She'd read enough to get a troubling picture of the patient named Selma and her boyfriend. The rest would have to wait for morning; she was simply too tired to read on.

As she picked up the file to reorganize the pages, something slipped out. A folded paper napkin with what appeared to be a telephone number written on it.

More interesting than the phone number was the name imprinted on the corner of the napkin. Pasquale's Ristorante.

The same little out-of-the-way café where Mark had taken her. Had he also taken the gorgeous Selma there? A cold fist closed around Sarah's heart.

At the same instant something crashed onto the balcony.

Chapter Five

Sarah could see nothing through the clammy curtain of fog. She opened the French doors and stepped into the damp chill of the night. "Who's there? Is somebody out there?"

Arms outstretched, she groped for the wooden rail and gripped it, straining to try to make out any object that might have been thrown onto the balcony.

In the distance a foghorn wailed mournfully. There was no other sound, but an acute sense of danger assailed her. There was somebody else on the balcony with her, she was certain of it.

She edged backward into the bedroom and quickly locked the French doors. Turning off the lights, she stood in the dark.

Had she detected a faint odor of tobacco smoke? Or was that the smell of Pacific fog?

No sound from outside. Between the intermittent moans of the foghorn the silence was overpowering. If there was a prowler, had he awakened either Harriet or Emma? With one hand on the wall Sarah felt her way around the room to the bedroom door. That morning she had bought several night-lights and she was grateful for the comforting glow as she crossed the landing to Emma's room.

The child seemed to be sleeping peacefully, with Mr. Buttons pressed to her cheek. Moving on, Sarah eased Harriet's door open and was reassured by the elderly woman's gentle snoring.

She closed the door and went downstairs, wondering if she dared go outside and look around. She was surrounded by uncovered windows. The gray fog pressed relentlessly against them. Although she couldn't see out, she was visible to any prowler. She unplugged the night-lights in the hall, leaving only those on the landing. Then she went up to the second floor living room and stood near the French doors, listening. Still nothing, but now the acrid stench of smoke was more pronounced.

Could she scare off the prowler by turning on the outside lights? A panel of switches near the front door controlled the porch and balcony lights. It took her a moment to pick her way carefully through the darkness to the front door.

As she neared it the gray fog that was visible through the frosted panes took on a dusty rose tint. It took her a moment to realize what was happening, then her heart pounded and she stumbled toward the door. The telephone began to ring shrilly.

She ignored it and flung open the door. Through the veil of mist she could see flames shooting out of the garage roof. Fire crackled and hissed, rapidly consuming the wooden structure.

For one horrified instant she stood watching, reliving the terror of the hotel bursting into flame. In that fire she'd lost everything that was dear to her—her parents and her fiancé. She gasped and then stumbled back inside, toward the ringing phone. But as soon as she picked up the receiver, the line went dead. Repeated jiggling failed to restore the dial tone. Switching on all the lights, she rushed outside again with some vague idea of turning the garden hose on the blaze. But the hose connection was frozen and refused to budge.

"Sarah!" Harriet's voice hailed her from the house. "Have you called the fire department?"

"No, the phone was dead!" *Maybe it's back on now.* "Dial 911!" she screamed over her shoulder as she tugged and pulled at the hose tap.

Then all at once capable hands pried the hose from her fingers and used a wrench to loosen the tap.

The shadowy figure beside her said, "At least there's no wind to blow sparks across the driveway to the house."

"Ben! Oh, thank God—here, give me the hose. My phone isn't working, you've got to call the fire department."

"I've already called them. People sometimes forget in the heat of the moment. Now why don't you go and get Harriet and Emma out of the house, just in case."

Sarah was carrying the sleepy child down the stairs when she heard the distant wail of sirens.

"THE INSURANCE COMPANY is going to love us," Sarah said as she and Ben sat in the kitchen drinking hot chocolate after the fire crew departed and Harriet and Emma were back in bed. "We not only burn down our garage, but destroy two cars. Not what you'd call a good track record considering we've only been here a couple of days."

Ben's eyebrows knitted together. "I'll drive you into town tomorrow and you can get a rental car."

"I don't know what would have happened if you hadn't seen the fire. We could have lost the house, too." She paused. "It's a miracle you did see the blaze through the fog."

"I heard a car coming down the hill and I knew it wasn't your Jeep."

"How did you know that?"

"It was traveling too fast. The tires were screaming, on the bends. I went outside, expecting to hear the car crash into the guardrail. That's when I looked up and saw the orange glow at the top of the hill. I called 911 and then tried to raise you. When you didn't answer the phone, I figured I'd better get up here."

"I didn't hear a car," Sarah mused. "The night seemed so quiet, with the fog. I couldn't even hear the surf."

"You're at the end of the peninsula, away from the road. If you sleep on the ocean side of the house, you won't hear cars. My place, on the other hand, is right by the road."

Sarah nodded. But she couldn't help wondering if Ben had in fact heard a car. How could the glow of the fire have been visible through the fog?

Ben leaned forward, his expression worried. "Sarah, the fire chief said for the flames to burn so fiercely there must have been flammable materials stored in the garage, probably set off by an electrical spark."

"I honestly don't know what was in there. Apart from getting the Jeep in and out, I haven't had time to check out what the previous owner left behind. He left a lot of stuff in the house, so I imagine those cabinets in the garage were full, too."

Sarah glanced at the kitchen clock. It was one-thirty. "Ben, I don't know how to thank you."

He stood up. "No need. I'd better go home so you can get some sleep. I guess Harriet and Emma must have settled down again."

"Emma didn't really wake up, thank goodness."

Sarah walked to the door with him. "Ben, do you smoke?"

"No. Why?"

"I thought I smelled cigarette smoke just before the fire started."

His jaw moved slightly. "And you thought maybe I started the fire just so I could rescue a damsel in distress?"

She flushed. "No, I didn't mean to imply—"

"Yes, you did. Look, Sarah, I'd be suspicious, too. There's nobody else on the hill but me. I could be an eccentric recluse who doesn't like sharing it, but I'm not. Or I could be madly attracted to you and trying to be a hero. While I won't deny you're extremely attractive, I would never put anyone in danger just so I could resort to phony heroics. Since we're being frank, I think it's fishy as hell that your husband's car was burned to ashes before an insurance investigator got a look at it."

Her pulse accelerated. "I hadn't thought of that. If the Mercedes was tampered with, as you believe the Jeep was . . ."

Ben nodded grimly. "And the Jeep's gone, too. If it wasn't the middle of the night, I'd be interested to hear just who your husband is . . . and what he was running from."

"Mark isn't running from anything," she managed to say, hoping it was true. "We came here because he wanted a quiet place to write a book."

"Uh-huh." Ben looked skeptical. "I know doctors and lawyers who want to write, but they don't usually give up their practices until they've made that first sale. Nor do they move clear across the country. How long have you two been married?"

Sarah hesitated before answering. "It will be four weeks tomorrow."

"How long did you know him before you were married?"

"For a few months, but if you say *marry in haste* I'll probably scream. I worked with my husband before we got married, so we were together a lot."

Ben shrugged. His eyes were full of compassion. "Working with somebody doesn't necessarily mean you're getting to know them. If I were you, I'd start asking questions. A lot of questions."

UNABLE TO SLEEP, Sarah almost wished she'd asked Ben to stay. She decided to find the insurance policies on the cars and the house. There was a built-in desk in the room Mark had chosen for his study and she supposed that's where Mark would have put such recently acquired papers.

Opening the top drawer of the desk she stared disbelievingly at a single sheet of paper. It was a month-to-month rental agreement for Cliff House, signed by Mark Lasiter as lessee and Clyde Vaughan as lessor. Mark had paid first and last month's rent and a security deposit.

In Sarah's exhausted state it took a moment for this revelation to sink in. Mark had told her he'd *bought* Cliff House. When she questioned him as to how he had accomplished the purchase so quickly, he'd replied that a private cash sale of a vacant house could go through in a matter of days.

She thought of the deed to the Long Island property. Did that mean he had not sold the house there? If so, why had he lied? Keeping the house on Long Island and renting this one indicated a temporary move. Did not telling his wife about it suggest that he considered her to be only temporary, too?

Sarah dozed fitfully until dawn, then got up and made a pot of strong coffee. Checking the phone, she was relieved to hear a dial tone. There was a telephone number on the rental agreement and she called it.

A cranky and ancient voice wheezed, "Vaughan. Who the hell's calling at this time of the morning?"

"Sarah Lasiter. My husband rented Cliff House from you."

"So? What do you want?"

"I'm afraid we've had a fire—the garage. The house wasn't touched."

She held the phone away from her ear as she was treated to a stream of salty expletives. When the man calmed down she added, "The fire chief believed you must have left quite a quantity of highly flammable materials in there."

"All I left in that garage was a bunch of old tools. Anything flammable *you* put in there lady."

"I've parked our cars in the garage, that's all. Perhaps you hadn't heard, my husband was in an accident. He's in a coma."

"If you want to get out of your agreement, you'll have to send me a month's written notice. Meantime, I'll call my insurance company."

The phone was slammed down in her ear.

Sarah looked up to see Harriet standing at the kitchen door.

"Is Emma awake?" Sarah asked.

"No."

"Good. Sit down, Harriet, I need to talk to you." Sarah put the rental agreement on the kitchen table in front of her, and then went to the refrigerator to get her a glass of orange juice. Returning with the glass she saw Harriet had pushed the rental agreement aside.

"Mark told me he bought this house," Sarah said.

"He probably intends to, but wanted to rent it for a while to see how it worked out."

"He didn't sell your Long Island house either, did he?"

Harriet avoided meeting her eyes.

"Is Mark running from something, Harriet? If he is you've got to tell me."

"He always wanted to write. That wasn't a sudden decision."

"But coming to California was." Sarah paused. "Marrying me was...."

"I was surprised by your whirlwind romance, and sudden marriage. You and Mark didn't know anything about each other. Of course you have questions about us—as we have about you."

"Then let's clear the air. What do you want to know about me?"

"Do you love my grandson?"

"Of course I do! What a question!"

"Please, look at the situation from my point of view. Mark is older than you, he's not only well-established in his profession, but also independently wealthy. Both his father and grandfather left him sizable estates."

"Did you ever ask him if he loved me? If we're looking for hidden agendas, you could also suggest that he might have wanted a mother for Emma." She didn't add that Harriet's advancing years and Emma's dependence on her might also have been a factor.

"That's an unromantic thing for a new bride to say, Sarah."

Sarah ran her hands distractedly through her hair. "I'm sorry. I guess what I'm trying to say is that we're drawn to people for many reasons, and Mark and I both had something to give each other beyond romantic love. But we were...are in love. And I do want to be a mother to Emma. But I realize now that there's so much I don't know about Mark's past. For instance, he's never told me anything about Tamara. Why did she leave?"

Harriet stared at her untouched glass of orange juice for an interminable minute. "We never talk about Tamara. Mark thought it best for Emma. She doesn't really remember her mother."

"But surely she's asked where her mother is? How can you not talk about her?"

Harriet shrugged her thin shoulders.

Sarah said, "I realize that Mark is the psychiatrist in the family, but don't you feel it's unwise to be so secretive about her mother?"

"No, I don't. Sarah, I think you're bringing up Mark's first wife because *you* are curious about her. If you wanted to know about her, you should have asked Mark before you two rushed into marriage."

"Yes, I realize that now. But since I don't have the option and several strange things have happened, I really need to know about her. I found some of Mark's personal papers, but I didn't see a divorce decree. Where is Tamara? Where did she go? Why doesn't she want to see her child?"

"I don't want to talk about Tamara. Sarah, Mark told me that your previous fiancé died on the day you were to be married. Do you think you somehow substituted Mark for your dead fiancé? That because you'd known *him* all your life, you didn't have to get to know Mark? Maybe you thought you could just have your happy ending."

Sarah let out her breath in a ragged sigh. Harriet's theory hit perilously close to home. "And do you have an explanation for why Mark wanted to marry me so quickly?"

"He'd been very lonely. You were good with Emma. You two had similar losses. But still, I thought he should have waited to get to know you better."

"Similar losses? My fiancé *died*."

"All right, Sarah, you want to know about Tamara? I'll tell you what my grandson should have told you. On the rare occasions he speaks of her he says she left, but the truth is, *she* died. He could never bring himself to say the word. He loved her so.''

The room swam for a second. ''Died? But...was it an accident? An illness?''

''Tamara committed suicide.''

Sarah felt as though she had been kicked in the chest. For a moment she couldn't speak. She thought rapidly. Emma had been almost two years old, surely Tamara would have been beyond post-partum depression by then? Had she had other problems?

''How...did she do it?''

''She hooked a hose to her car's exhaust.''

''At the Long Island house?''

''No. She drove to her mother's house. Her mother was away, spending the winter in Florida. Tamara had gone off by herself before, several times. She was always threatening to leave. I suppose that's why Mark says she left him. Nobody thought to check her mother's garage until... well, the body wasn't found for a while.''

Harriet was very pale and Sarah could see her hands were shaking. Feeling guilty for forcing the older woman to re-live what must have been an extremely painful period, Sarah jumped up and ran around the table. Slipping her arm around the frail shoulders she murmured, ''I'm so sorry. How awful, for all of you. I understand now why Mark doesn't want to talk about it. Maybe it would be best if Emma never found out.''

Feeling Harriet tense at her touch, Sarah abruptly withdrew her arm. She picked up the coffeepot and filled two cups. Now that the initial shock at the revelation of Tamara's suicide was wearing off, Sarah wondered if Mark should have felt morally or ethically bound to disclose his first wife's suicide to her before he'd asked her to marry him.

"I take it that Tamara's mother doesn't want to play any role in Emma's life? How sad. She is her grandmother, after all."

"She died, too," Harriet said in a strangely flat tone. "Only a few weeks after Tamara. Sarah, when Mark comes home, you won't let him know I told you..." She looked over Sarah's shoulder. "Morning honey, you want some juice?"

Emma padded into the room.

"Hi, Emma," Sarah said brightly. "How'd you like some pancakes for breakfast? I bought some boysenberry syrup."

Emma's lower lip trembled. "My Daddy burned up, din' he?"

"Oh, no, angel!" Sarah was aghast. "The garage and the cars burned, that's all."

Emma buried her face in Harriet's arm.

Resigned, Sarah said, "All right. We'll go to the hospital to see your Daddy."

Chapter Six

Ben Travis arrived shortly after nine o'clock, driving a minivan, and showed no surprise when he saw that all three of them were going into town. Sarah avoided looking at the charred shell of the garage and the sinister skeletons of the two cars as she lifted Emma into Ben's back seat.

"We're going to the hospital," Sarah explained as they started down the hill. "Emma wants to see her daddy."

Ben glanced sideways at her. "Tough call."

Sarah nodded.

In the back seat Harriet put her arm around Emma and stared out at the sullen gray ocean, roiling under a pewter sky.

Sarah asked Ben, "Do you know a man named Clyde Vaughan?"

"Old Cap'n Vaughan? Sure. He's the former owner of Cliff House."

"He's the *present* owner of Cliff House," Sarah corrected.

"But I thought—"

"So did I. Ben, do you have business in town, or are you being Mr. Good Samaritan again?"

"I was going to stop by the gallery and then pick up some art supplies. Nothing that won't keep. Why?"

"I was wondering if you'd mind driving Harriet and Emma home later. After I pick up a rental car, I'm going to see Captain Vaughan."

"Sure, be glad to."

"I'll have to get the doctor's permission for Emma to go into intensive care, since they don't usually allow kids to visit. Perhaps you could go to the gallery while I deal with the hospital?"

"Sure." Moments later, Ben dropped them at the entrance to the hospital, and they walked into a plant-filled lobby. A few early visitors sat on vinyl couches, leafing through magazines or staring into space. Two walls were brightened by enormous acrylic paintings of whales and dolphins swimming in an underwater jungle. Ben's work had an uplifting quality, a feeling of freedom and motion and joy.

Sarah led the way along a hushed corridor to the elevators. The doors to ICU were kept locked and it was necessary for a nurse to check through a glass panel to be sure any visitors were authorized before buzzing them in. Only adult immediate family members were permitted.

Sarah lifted Emma into her arms and mouthed through the glass, "She needs to see her daddy."

The nurse walked over to the door, unlocked it and slid outside. "I'm sorry, Mrs. Lasiter, children aren't allowed in ICU."

"Just for a moment? She doesn't believe he's here, she thinks he's left her. I'll hold her. I promise she won't touch him—or anything else."

The nurse nodded sympathetically. "All right, you can come in for a minute. Your husband's the only patient in here today."

"Thanks," Sarah said, sincerely grateful. "You remember the other Mrs. Lasiter, don't you? My husband's grandmother."

"Sure. You can all go in, but please don't stay too long, or I'll be in big trouble."

Sarah stopped at the foot of Mark's bed. "See honey, there's your daddy. He's sleeping."

Emma gave one wide-eyed glance at her father's bandaged head, his bruised and battered face trailing plastic tubes, and the battery of blinking monitors, then buried her head in Sarah's shoulder.

"It's all right, baby," Sarah murmured soothingly, stroking the child's silky hair. "The machines are helping Daddy feel better."

"You'd better take her back to the waiting room," Harriet said in a brittle voice that threatened to shatter into tears. "I'll stay with Mark just for a moment."

On their way out, the nurse smiled sympathetically and said, "I'm sorry we couldn't let Dr. Lasiter's sister in a little while ago, but his doctor was with him at the time. I did tell her she could wait, but she got mad and left."

"Sister?" Sarah felt a stab of alarm. "Did you check her ID?"

"Well, no, as I said, she couldn't go in just then anyway, because the doctor wasn't finished."

"Mark doesn't have a sister. He has no relatives other than his grandmother and daughter." Sarah's mind raced. Who would have visited Mark? "What did the woman look like?"

The nurse frowned. "Sort of ordinary. Dark hair, glasses."

At least she didn't sound like the blond Mae Peterson, Sarah thought . . . unless the woman had worn a wig and prop glasses.

"I'd better have a word with the doctor," Sarah said. "Please don't let anyone other than Mrs. Lasiter senior and myself in, okay?"

SARAH TRIED TO HIDE her anxiety from Harriet and Emma as they waited in the lobby for Ben to return to pick them up. Emma did not seem reassured that her father was being cared for. Sarah held her and rocked gently back and forth, trying to get her to look at Ben's paintings.

Harriet seemed to have sunk into deep depression after visiting her grandson. "I outlived my only son," she said heavily, "please God, I can't outlive my grandson, too."

Sarah shot her an exasperated message with her eyes. *Please be careful what you say in front of Emma.* Aloud she said firmly, "Emma's daddy will be coming home soon. We have to think good thoughts and say lots of prayers."

"Did you talk to his doctor?"

"Yes. He said Mark could come out of the coma at any time." Sarah had also alerted the doctor to the mythical sister. She'd been assured that only she and Harriet would be admitted to see Mark.

But who was the woman? To Sarah's knowledge, Mark knew no one in California. Of course she was beginning to realize that there was much about her husband's behavior that was baffling, and much that he hadn't confided in her.

Along with unanswered questions, Mae Peterson hovered, specterlike, at the back of Sarah's mind. Perhaps it was time to track her down and ask a few questions. Sarah was relieved to see Ben's broad shoulders and tousled head rising above an approaching group of visitors.

"You ladies ready to head for the hills?" He reached into his inside jacket pocket to produce a box of crayons and a coloring book. "I thought a certain little girl could use these."

"Thank you," Sarah said, taking the gifts and handing them to Harriet. Emma might have been in a trance for all the attention she paid to any of them.

Ben looked at her questioningly and Sarah added, "She's upset—her Daddy was hurt, but he's going to be all right."

Sarah carried the child out to Ben's van. Twenty minutes later he pulled into a car rental agency. Sarah kissed Emma's cheek. "I'll see you later, angel."

She hated to leave the child, but felt a rising sense of urgency to track down Mae Peterson. The conversation with her landlord would have to wait, she decided, as she rented a Ford.

Emerald Cove was little more than a fishing village set on the picturesque coastline. It had never been popular with beachgoers due to the lack of sandy beaches, treacherous undersea rocks, and vicious rip currents. The small private hospital was probably the most important building in town. Sarah drove the rented car down Main Street until she spotted a real estate office, parked and went inside.

A middle-aged woman with a leathery tan and white-blond hair was seated at one of two desks. Her face broke into a welcoming smile as Sarah entered the office. "Good morning. My name's Bess Miller. Can I help you?"

"Hi, I'm Sarah Lasiter. We're renting Cliff House."

The smile was instantly replaced with a sympathetic frown. "Oh, Mrs. Lasiter, what a time you've had! First your husband's accident, then a fire. I don't blame you for wanting to move out of that old white elephant of a house. I hope your husband didn't sign a lease?"

"No, we're on a month-to-month rental."

"Good. Your thirty-day notice will cover your escrow period, as soon as we find you a place."

"Ms. Miller, I'm not ready to look for another place to live yet, although in the future we might. I wondered if you had a woman named Mae Peterson working here. She came from Las Vegas, Nevada, I'm not sure when.''

Bess Miller's eyes rolled. "Emerald Cove Realty consists of one broker—me. I don't have any agents currently. I've hardly done enough business to support myself since the recession hit. There's another real estate office at the south end of town, run by two brothers who made a mint in the eighties and just keep the office open to get away from their wives. No Mae Peterson there, either. You sure she's selling real estate? She'd have to have a California license.''

"No, I'm not sure of anything. How many hotels and motels are there?"

"In town? There's the bed-and-breakfast inn and the old downtown hotel. Nearest motel is way out, east of the highway. Why don't you sit down and call them? I'll get you a cup of coffee."

"Thanks, that's kind of you."

Bess Miller grinned. "Hey, I've got to keep you warm until you're ready to buy a place. Prospects are few and far between.''

Sarah quickly ascertained that there was no Mae Peterson registered anywhere in the vicinity of Emerald Cove. She thanked Bess again, got directions to Clyde Vaughan's house and drove ten miles east to a retirement community beside a golf course.

She had worked herself up into a confrontational mood, fearing her landlord might refuse to talk to her after his terseness on the phone. When the door to a small stucco house was opened by a wizened gnome of a man and she gave her name, his tiny bright eyes went over her from head to toe.

"You're pretty," he said. "You can come in. How come you didn't come with your husband when he was looking for a place to live? I told him he should've let you see Cliff House before he rented it. Women never like the place.''

She followed him into a small living room that was jammed with more souvenirs from his maritime years. Little wonder he'd left so much behind at Cliff House.

''I was in New York,'' Sarah answered, accepting the chair he offered.

''Called my insurance agent. Somebody'll be out to look at the fire damage either today or tomorrow.''

''Thank you. Captain Vaughan, I was wondering how you and my husband met.''

''He answered my ad, a'course. It was an old one—been up on the bulletin board at the grocery store for months. Never thought anybody would ever call on it. Almost forgot I'd put it there. Had the place listed with Bess Miller for a year or so before that. Figured I'd cut the price by the amount of the commission, maybe unload it that way. Couldn't take care of it any more. Getting up in years and couldn't handle all the stairs. Tried to talk your husband into buying it, or at least into taking a lease-option, but he wouldn't go for it.''

''So you had an ad saying you wanted to sell, but my husband came and offered to rent?''

''That's right. I figured at least somebody would be there to keep an eye on the place. Reckon you want to hand me a month's notice now, huh?''

''No, no I don't.''

''That's a relief. Sorry I cussed you out on the phone. I heard you city folks like to sue people at the drop of a hat. I was worried you were setting me up with all that talk of flammable material in the garage.''

''Captain Vaughan, I haven't seen my husband—not conscious anyway—since he said goodbye to me in New York a week before his accident. I was wondering if he said anything to you about how long he planned to rent the house, or stay in Emerald Cove?''

Vaughan shook his head. ''Paid me cash and took the keys.'' He gave her a crafty glance. ''Didn't tell you what he was up to either, huh?''

He sure hadn't. Was there no one she could trust? Unbidden the image of Ben's craggy features came to mind. ''I thought we'd bought the house and planned to stay permanently,'' she said. ''Finding the rental agreement was a surprise. Did he say *anything* about his plans?''

''Nope. He was just kinda eager to close the deal. Said he liked the place but if I wouldn't let him move right in, he'd lined up a couple of other places.''

''And that was the last time you spoke to him?''

''That's right. I'd have called and told him his sister was looking for him but the phone wasn't in yet.''

Sarah felt the blood drain from her face. ''His sister?''

''Uh-huh. Don't recall her name. She calls me and sez she's got to get in touch on account of a family emergency. Said she was calling from some rental storage kind of place. Somebody in town had told her Dr. Lasiter checked out of the bed-and-breakfast inn and moved into a property of mine.''

''And you gave her the address and directions to Cliff House?'' Sarah asked in a hollow voice.

He nodded.

''Did you ever meet this woman?''

''Nope. Just spoke to her on the phone.''

''Did she say what the emergency was?''

''Uh-huh. Said his little girl had been in an accident.''

''Look, I'm not asking for her address,'' Sarah said. ''All I'm asking is that you call her and tell her I want to talk to her. I'd call her myself but apparently her phone is un-listed.''

The young receptionist at Help-U-Rent squirmed ner-vously. ''I'm not supposed to give out information on our clients.''

''You wouldn't be,'' Sarah said as patiently as she was able. ''You'd be telling her about me.''

''She didn't come to us for a place to rent,'' the recep-tionist whispered at length. ''Try A-1 Summer Rentals on Seaview.''

At A-1 Summer Rentals and Stationery Supplies the manager was more cooperative. He unloaded boxes of computer paper and listened to Sarah's story. She ex-plained that her husband's sister had preceded them to Emerald Cove and she had inadvertently lost her address and phone number. Finally, the man picked up the phone and dialed.

''Ms. Peterson? This is Al at A-1 Rentals. I've got a Mrs. Lasiter in the office. She wanted your address and phone number.''

Sarah strained to hear what was being said on the other end of the line, but Mae Peterson's response was unintelli-gible.

Al replaced the receiver. ''She'll meet you at the pier in half an hour. Said she's on her way to buy some fish.''

''Thank you,'' Sarah said.

Twenty minutes later she parked the rental car at the end of the pier and stepped out into a bitingly cold wind.

A black Porsche with Nevada license plates was the only other car parked adjacent to the pier. There was a slight dent and a few scratches on the hood. Sarah was pretty sure it was the car Mae Peterson had been in when it hit the guardrail.

Fishing boats and pleasure craft bobbed at their moorings and she could see a couple of men hauling their catch into a large wooden shed at the end of the pier, but she appeared to be the only woman walking out along the weathered wood planks. Once again, she thought of Ben. This time she wished he'd come with her.

When she reached the shed, she saw Mae Peterson standing inside smoking a cigarette. The woman stubbed it out on the floor. "Oh, hi, Mrs. Lasiter. How's the doctor?"

"About the same. Do you think we could go somewhere and talk? It's so cold out here by the ocean."

"Sure. Hang on a second while I get my fish. I love fresh fish, how about you?"

Sarah waited as Mae walked over to a long marble slab where an apron-clad man was piling fish. When Mae pointed to her selection the man reached for a lethal-looking knife in order to clean the fish, but Mae murmured something to him and he handed the knife to her.

Mae then walked around to the other side of the marble counter and, grinning at Sarah, positioned the fish in front of her. She fingered the edge of the knife, adjusted the fish, raised the knife experimentally, lowered it, paused and raised it again.

Sarah's whole body froze. *She's acting like she's preparing for an execution and I'm to be a witness.*

The knife flashed downward, beheading the fish.

Sarah turned away at the sound of steel striking marble and began to walk in the other direction. She was joined minutes later by Mae Peterson, who now had a package under her arm. "Let's go. I'll drop off the fish in my fridge and meet you at Tilly's—that's the little café on Main Street."

Feeling vaguely queasy, Sarah nodded and hurried back to her car. Since they could have met at the café in the first place, it seemed Mae had wanted to put on the little show with the fish for her. Why? To show her skill with a chopping blade? To scare her?

For the first time Sarah considered the possibility that the woman who called herself Mae Peterson might have a mental disorder.

Mark was a psychiatrist. Had he treated her? If so, could she have formed a one-sided attachment to him? Sarah knew this was a common problem psychiatrists and psychologists faced.

She buckled her seat belt in the Ford and waited for Mae to start the Porsche. The windshield was tinted and she couldn't see her expression, but the car remained stationary. After a moment Sarah turned on her ignition and pulled out. The Porsche immediately roared to life.

As Sarah started to drive the winding road back to town, Mae positioned the Porsche inches from her back bumper and kept it there despite the fact that Sarah changed speeds frequently and slowed almost to a stop for the tightest curves.

By the time the gas station at the edge of the town came into view, Sarah's nerves were strung so tight that she gripped the wheel with frozen fingers. On an impulse, she swung into the gas station, intending to confront Mae about her reckless tailgating.

The Porsche roared past and disappeared.

Sarah waited a few minutes, then drove into town.

There was no sign of Mae Peterson at Tilly's Café. Sarah waited half an hour, then gave up and went home.

Chapter Seven

The phone line to Las Vegas was filled with static, probably due to another Pacific storm moving in. Sarah repeated, "I want the number of the Board of Realtors—or some other organization that can tell me about a real estate agent. I don't know which broker she worked for and I need some information about her."

Two calls later, she was given the name of a well-known franchise. A woman answered the phone and Sarah asked if Mae Peterson was, or had been, one of their agents.

"Sure. One of our best," the disembodied voice responded.

Sarah almost dropped the receiver in surprise. Of all the comments she had expected, this had not been on the list.

"Is she currently working for you?"

"Yes, but she's on a leave of absence. Can someone else help you?"

"No, thank you."

Sarah put down the phone and stared at it, trying to make sense out of her wild ride from the pier into town and futile wait at the café. Mae Peterson really was from Las Vegas, Nevada. How could she possibly have known Mark previously? What had really brought her to their door the other night, and what had prompted her interest in them?

The doorbell rang and she jumped up, thinking perhaps it was Ben. Hoping it was Ben. He seemed to be a bulwark of strength in an increasingly hostile environment.

But it wasn't Ben.

It was Mae Peterson, carrying a bunch of dried flowers and wearing an apologetic grin. "Hey, Mrs. L., I hope I didn't scare you, I was just trying to take your mind off your troubles. And I'm real sorry I couldn't make it to the café—durn Porsche conked out on me. Hope you didn't wait too long."

Sarah thought rapidly. Both Emma and Harriet were upstairs taking a nap. They were tired after their interrupted sleep the previous night. "Come in," Sarah said, unhooking the chain on the door.

"What happened to your garage?" Mae asked as she followed her into the kitchen. "You have a fire or something?"

"Please, sit down." Sarah indicated a chair on the far side of the table, wanting a barricade between them.

"I brought these for you." Mae put the flowers on the table. She looked around. This is some weird house."

"Miss Peterson—"

"Call me Mae, please. And I'll call you Sarah."

"What do you want from me, Mae?"

Pale eyebrows went up in dismayed surprise. "Want from you? Nothing. I'm trying to show my gratitude, that's all."

"And that futile trip out to the pier and wild ride to town, not to mention leaving me waiting at the café—that was your idea of gratitude?"

"I thought you'd like to see the pier, maybe buy some fish. Who knew it would be so cold and breezy?"

"Perhaps the fact that it's January might have given us a hint?"

"I thought California was supposed to be warm and sunny all the time."

"You're thinking of *southern* California, and even there they have cold rainy days this time of year."

"Well, I'm sorry. What can I do to make it up to you?"

"You can tell me why you lied about owning the Porsche."

"I didn't lie. It isn't my car. It belongs to a friend. I own the Mercedes I drove up to your place the next day. Real estate clients like to ride in comfort you know, and a car like that says I'm successful at what I do. Inspires confidence. The only reason I have the Porsche today is because I'm supposed to be taking it in to get the body work done. You know, the dents and scratches where we hit the guardrail. But then you called and wanted to see me, so I had to change my plans."

"All right, now tell me why you went to the hospital and pretended to be my husband's sister."

Pale gray eyes widened in apparent astonishment. "Somebody did that? You're kidding! You want me to go back there with you to prove it wasn't me?"

Sarah swallowed hard. "I don't suppose you called our landlord, either?"

Mae shook her head vehemently. With her pale hair, almost colorless eyes and chalk white complexion she was unnervingly wraithlike and Sarah had the eerie feeling she was battling a ghost.

"Then how did you know about us? Our name—my husband's profession?"

"My friend mentioned that a doctor named Lasiter had moved into Cliff House, that night we hit the guard rail."

"Why were you driving up the cliff road anyway? Where were you going?"

Mae smirked. "We were going to park. Crazy, huh? But we just felt like acting like kids that night. We thought we'd drive to the top of the cliff and watch the storm."

"And who is this friend of yours? His car has Nevada plates, so how did he know about us?"

"Boy, this is some interrogation, Sarah. If you must know he's from Las Vegas, but he has a summer place in Emerald Cove. He is also very much married. That's why I didn't want to make a big deal out of hitting the guardrail that night. I just wanted to keep a low profile, you know?"

Sarah realized she was still standing, and she sank into a chair. Everything Mae had said sounded reasonable, and yet...

"Where was your friend when we went back to the Porsche after you hit the rail then? You said he was hurt, bleeding."

"It was just a nosebleed. He bumped his face on the wheel. A lot of blood, you know, but not much damage. He was knocked out for a minute, then came to and walked down the hill and hitched a ride to town. He thought the Porsche was tangled up in the guardrail and couldn't be driven. We were both pretty shook up that night, you know."

Mae leaned forward. "Look, I realize you must be feeling pretty suspicious, what with somebody claiming to be your sister-in-law and all. But honestly, I'd just like to be your friend. It sounds like you could use one, between a fake family member and a mysterious fire. Who knows what's next, huh?"

The implied threat hung in the air, and Sarah suppressed a shiver as she gazed into transparent eyes that were like mirrors, showing no emotion, yet reflecting Sarah's own fears back to her.

The doorbell rang, breaking the tension. Sarah stood up. "That's probably the insurance adjuster. Will you excuse me now?"

"Sure. I'll let him in on my way out." Mae picked up her purse and strolled from the room.

Sarah paused. The dried flowers lay on the table, dead and sinister, and she picked them up and thrust them into the trash bin beneath the sink. Then she went to speak to the insurance adjuster, and to make sure Mae Peterson had truly left.

LATE THAT NIGHT, Sarah pored over Mark's notes. She needed to get her mind off the mysterious Mae. Even worse, off Ben Travis. Like it or not she was attracted to him—and the emotions made her feel disloyal. Mark's handwritten manuscript was scored with corrections and crossed-out passages and some pages had questions written in the margins. She studied the margin notes on a closely written page.

Brief reactive psychosis?

Disorders of impulse control?

Dissociative disorder?

Psychosexual disorder? But doesn't the word disorder recognize that some behaviors may be endogenous?

Sarah stopped to look up the last word in a dictionary. Endogenous: arising from within the individual.

There were several other notations that were either indecipherable or meaningless to her, so she concentrated on the main text.

The afternoon was hot. A sultry stillness pervaded, lulling me into an almost hypnotic trance as I waited for Selma to continue. Paradoxically, the atmosphere between us throbbed with an electric tension.

I wanted to get up and turn up the air-conditioning, fling open a window, suck in great gulps of air. But I couldn't find the energy to even loosen my collar.

Selma uncrossed her legs. I heard the sound of her bare flesh peel away from the leather chair and kept my gaze fastened on her face.

The subtle hint of musk lingered, making me want to breathe more deeply, to inhale the fragrance that I was sure was hers alone.

A bead of perspiration glistened on her upper lip and she fanned herself with what appeared to be a theater program. The invitation in her eyes was unmistakable.

I heard a distant drumming in my ears and felt primitive urges pluck at nerve endings. My blood churned. All at once I was as aware of my own body as a moment before I had been of hers. I had lost all professional detachment and the worst part of it was . . . I didn't care.

Sarah put down the page, feeling keyed up, tense in a way she didn't want to define; wanting to read on yet afraid to, wanting to believe that the fictional Matt Layton was the one lusting for his patient, not her husband, not Mark.

He had switched to first person again, she realized. Perhaps that was what gave the description of the session the uncomfortable ring of realism. But even if the scene had come from Mark's imagination, she was still disturbed by the eroticism of his thoughts. Had he ever really reacted to a patient that way? Surely, his professional ethics would never have allowed it.

The bedroom was cold, and outside the wind was again buffeting the house. She felt stifled, claustrophobic, more alone than she had ever been before. She wished she could get into the car and drive into town, to see lights, hear music, to be with people. Maybe even Ben. But she couldn't leave Emma and Harriet alone.

Still, she had to get out into the fresh air. She needed to think. Pushing the notes back into the file, she stood up and went into the closet. After returning the file to the shelf, she put on her parka, pulled up the hood, and went out through the French doors to the balcony.

Icy blasts of brine-scented air knifed into her lungs. The marine layer had settled over the ocean and gray tendrils of cloud crept over the cliffs. There was no moon, or stars. She longed for light, yearned for human sounds, but could hear only the rhythmic push and pull of the surf against the rocks below.

Drawing a deep breath, she went back inside, kicked off her shoes and crawled into bed, still wearing the parka. She felt as if she would never be warm again.

SARAH'S SLEEP WAS FITFUL. She dreamed she was uncomfortably hot. She was back in Mark's office in Manhattan, working at her computer while he conducted a session with a patient.

In the dream she gradually realized she was naked. She tried to cover herself as she rose and moved, leaden-limbed, to the door of Mark's private office. When she tried to open his door, it refused to budge.

She wanted to call to him to come and let her in, but she couldn't make a sound. At length she turned away. She saw then that her desk was covered with bouquets of dried flowers.

Someone was pounding on the office door, but she daren't let them in. She was naked. Besides, she had to get rid of those sinister dried flowers.

She cried out as a hand closed around her shoulder, shaking her.

"Sarah, wake up. Ben's here. He wants to talk to you and he says it can't wait."

She blinked Harriet into focus. "What? What time is it?"

"Nearly nine—you slept late. I didn't want to wake you because I heard you up real late last night. But Ben seems quite perturbed."

Sarah sat up. "Tell him I'll be right down."

The sun was shining this morning and as she hurriedly donned jeans and a sweater her fears of the previous night evaporated. She ran a brush through her hair, then went downstairs.

Ben was in the kitchen with Emma, who watched with solemn concentration as he sketched colorful animals with her crayons onto a paper napkin. They hadn't seen Sarah approach. As he held up the napkin to display a sea lion frolicking with a beach ball, Sarah suddenly remembered the napkin she had found with Mark's notes, the one from Pasquale's with a telephone number written on it. Perhaps later she'd call that number.

Emma saw her then and smiled. "You're a sleepyhead!"

"Yes, I am." Sarah ruffled the child's honey-colored curls. "Did you have breakfast?"

"Oh, yes, a long time ago. Nana made scrambled eggs."

"Good morning, Ben," Sarah said. "How about you, have you eaten yet?"

His expression was grave. He rolled his eyes toward the door. "Could we talk?"

"Let's go into the captain's mess."

On the way she explained, "That's what Mark called the room that I suppose Captain Vaughan used as a study."

Ben closed the door carefully and then turned to face her. "A man's body has been found, wedged into the rocks just below the lookout point."

Chapter Eight

"Who is he?" Sarah asked. "How did he die?"

"I don't know," Ben said. "I heard a rescue truck go up the hill at dawn, and watched them haul a stretcher up the cliff. A little while later the coroner and the cops arrived. One of them came to ask if I'd seen anyone or heard anything. Because there was no wrecked vehicle, they think it might have been a hiker. The cop said the guy probably went over the cliff about a week ago. I told them I just got back from San Francisco. I could see they were stringing yellow crime scene tape, so I came to warn you that you'll probably have a visit from the cops any minute."

"I'd better have Harriet take Emma upstairs and keep her out of the way. The poor baby is already scared to death. She doesn't need to hear about this."

Sarah moved toward the door, but Ben caught her arm. "In spite of what the cop said, the yellow tape makes me think they believe they had a homicide. And if the body has been down there for several days... well, the man could have been killed about the time of your husband's accident."

Sarah tensed. "What are you implying, Ben?"

"Maybe I'd better tell you that I made some inquiries around town yesterday. The day your husband arrived in Emerald Cove he asked if there was a gun shop in town."

Sarah bristled. "He probably just wanted the gun for protection up here. We are completely isolated, after all."

"Your husband also didn't stay in one place for long. He checked into the bed-and-breakfast, then abruptly moved to the hotel, then back to the B-and-B. The last couple of nights before his accident nobody saw him so they presume he slept at Cliff House."

"What business is it of yours where Mark stayed? Just what is your interest in my husband?"

"My interest, Sarah, is in your safety. Somebody tampers with your car. Your garage mysteriously burns down. It sure looks like trouble followed you here. I don't know your husband, but I asked myself why any guy would bring a pretty young bride, a little daughter, and an elderly grandmother to as remote a place as Cliff House."

"I told you. He wants to write—"

"Look, I know your husband's in the hospital . . ." Ben paused. "But he could write back East. Come on, Sarah. Take off the blinders. Your husband came here to hide out from somebody, but it looks as if they found him. Furthermore, it looks like now they're after the rest of his family."

"You'd better go,' Sarah said curtly. "I'd like to at least have a cup of coffee before the police arrive."

But the police didn't come. Sarah waited, growing increasingly more nervous. She called the hospital, but there was no change in Mark's condition. She told Harriet about the discovery of the body and asked her to take Emma upstairs when the police arrived. She would have liked to ask Harriet more questions about Mark's past, but she didn't want to do so in front of Emma.

She busied herself unpacking suitcases and boxes, sweeping and dusting, pausing frequently to attempt to chat with Emma. But the child answered in monosyllables and spent the morning simply clutching Mr. Buttons.

"She usually watches 'Sesame Street' at about this time," Harriet offered.

"I'll buy a TV when I have time and get somebody to put in a jack and an antenna or whatever it is that makes them work," Sarah answered. "Harriet, while we're on the subject, why didn't Mark ship the furniture and appliances out here?"

Harriet shrugged her frail shoulders. "I think he wanted you to choose your own." Her eyes didn't meet Sarah's.

"He didn't sell the Long Island house, did he?"

Harriet didn't respond for a moment, then she said, "Not yet. But it's still on the market. The real estate agent thought the house would show better furnished."

It was a reasonable explanation, but Sarah persisted, "Is it possible Mark hoped to go back there someday?"

Harriet fixed Sarah with an icy stare. "My grandson didn't confide his future plans in me. He stopped telling me what he was going to do the day he started seeing you.

"That was not my wish, Harriet," Sarah retorted.

"I didn't say it was. But you must admit there was a secretiveness to your affair—"

"Affair! We weren't having an affair."

"Did you sleep together before you were married?"

"Oh, come on, this is the nineties!"

"You're entire...courtship was conducted secretly. I met you only once, on Emma's birthday. None of our friends had any social contact with you. In fact, it seemed that Mark went to great lengths to keep your real relationship from becoming known to anyone, including me. Then all of a sudden Mark married you and we had to sell the house—a house incidentally that was built by Mark's father."

"Again, not my idea. But come to think of it, I never stayed for more than a couple of hours at your house on Long Island. And I was never invited to meet any of your friends, so don't blame me for what you think of as our reclusiveness. Frankly, I'm beginning to wonder just what was going on in Mark's life the last weeks before we left New York."

"Oh, Sarah." Harriet sighed. "My dear, is it possible that Mark was having second thoughts about marrying you? That he was afraid you wouldn't fit in with the scheme of his life, so he had to make a new one with you? No, don't look at me like that. I know that sounds snobbish, but Mark is—what? At least fifteen years older than you, and from a highly privileged background."

In the brief silence that fell, Emma gave a slight sniffle. Sarah said quickly, "It's all right, honey, Nana and I aren't quarreling."

Sarah began to furiously scrub the sink. At least she now knew where she really stood with Mark's grandmother. Harriet apparently felt Sarah wasn't good enough for her grandson.

Just before noon the doorbell rang. The blue uniform of the Emerald Cove Police Department was visible through the frosted-glass panel of the front door. Sarah waited until Harriet had ushered Emma upstairs before she responded.

The young officer she showed into the living room lost no time in getting to the point.

"A man's body was found not far from the location of your husband's accident. There's no wrecked vehicle. We think there's a chance he might have been with your husband that night, but there's no ID on the body. Could you tell us if you have any thoughts on who else might have been in the car?''

Sarah shook her head. "I don't believe Mark knew anybody locally."

"The man appears to be in his early fifties, about five-nine, hundred and seventy pounds, gray hair."

"Sorry. I don't know anybody who fits that description."

"Mrs. Lasiter, we really need some help in identifying the body. Would you mind looking at a picture of the man? Perhaps you'll recognize him as being somebody known to your husband."

He didn't wait for a response, and Sarah found herself looking at a Polaroid of the dead man. Apart from the effects of exposure, the features were not visibly traumatized, but she couldn't help but notice that the dead man's eyes were wide and staring, registering pure terror.

She turned away quickly. "No, I don't know who he is."

ON HER WAY TO the hospital that afternoon, Sarah prayed that Mark would have come out of the coma and would be able to allay her fears. She drove slowly past the yellow-taped area near the lookout point. All of the law enforcement vehicles had left and there was nothing to see.

There was no guardrail below the point where Mark's car had gone over the cliff, but despite the recent heavy rains the skid marks he'd left were still visible. She cruised slowly around the long curve, wishing there was a safe place to stop and look down at the stand of twisted pines that had finally stopped the deadly plunge of his car.

She could understand how a highway patrolman on the Coast Highway below could have observed Mark's car crashing over the cliff, but who had spotted a man's body down there days later?

At the hospital there was no change in Mark's condition. Sarah stayed with him for an hour, then, needing groceries and having run out of ready cash, she decided to go to the bank.

She went to a counter marked New Accounts and introduced herself to a bubbly young woman. "My husband, Dr. Mark Lasiter, recently opened an account here." She gave both the Cliff House address and Mark's Long Island address. "But my husband had an accident. He's in a coma and I don't know what he did with either the checkbook or passbook."

The wooden nameplate on the new accounts desk proclaimed Miss Bubbly to be Kim Osborne. "Oh, yes, I read about the accident. I'm so sorry, how is your husband?"

"No change, I'm afraid. Would you mind looking up his account and issuing some temporary checks?"

"Sure, no problem. Just have a seat and I'll be right back."

Kim Osborne returned moments later, now wearing an apologetic smile. "I'm sorry, I forgot to ask for some ID."

Sarah felt her heart sink. She had obtained her driver's license before her marriage, so it was in her maiden name. She had nothing showing her married name. She explained this to Kim Osborne, who nodded sympathetically.

"Sure, I understand. But we don't have your signature card on file. I wish there was something I could do."

"Would it help if I brought in my marriage certificate?"

Kim brightened. "Sounds like a plan. Let me put it to my manager." She disappeared again.

Minutes passed before she returned, this time accompanied by a portly man who regarded Sarah suspiciously over tortoiseshell half glasses. "I'm sorry, Mrs. Lasiter, we have no record of your husband opening any accounts with this bank."

Sarah blinked. "But isn't this the only bank in town?"

"Yes, it is."

The man went into a lengthy discourse on where she could find other banks, but Sarah wasn't listening. She excused herself and left. She had closed out her own accounts before leaving New York and had only a few dollars left in her purse. *Damn,* she thought, *I'll have to ask Harriet for money.*

Leaving the bank, she saw a familiar figure crossing the street toward her. Ben waved and closed the distance between them in a few long strides. "Hi, Sarah. Did the cops talk to you?"

"Yes. They also showed me a picture of the dead man. I didn't know him." A biting wind almost took her breath away.

"Where are you headed?"

"Home, if you can call it that."

"Let me buy you a cup of coffee first, you look frozen to the bone."

"I really should get back—"

"Come on, the drive up the cliff will go easier if you have a little caffeine in you."

He ushered her half a block to a tiny combination bakery and coffee shop with two small tables in front of the counter. Sarah sat down as he ordered coffee and orange muffins in what to Sarah was an unnecessarily loud voice. He waited at the counter until the middle-aged woman handed him a tray with his order.

When he joined Sarah she asked, "Aren't we inviting gossip?"

"Probably. Do you care?"

"I should. But I'd really like to know what else you found out about my husband's activities last week. That is, if you can speak in a whisper."

Ben glanced back at the counter. The woman who had waited on him had disappeared into the back of the store. "She's deaf as a post, that's why I brought you here."

"I hope that doesn't mean you have something awful to tell me."

"No, I just wanted to talk to you alone—out of earshot of Harriet and Emma. Have you figured out what was going on with your husband?"

She shrugged. "Nothing's going on."

"Okay, so tell me what you really think about being dropped down on this part of the coast. It must be a real contrast to what you've been used to."

She smiled wryly. "We're talking major culture shock. I feel as if I've been banished to the dark side of the moon. I loved my life in New York. I loved the city—the energy, the excitement, the people. Every day was an adventure."

"Then why did you agree to relocate?"

Sarah bit her lip. "The life I loved ended a year ago, when my parents and fiancé were killed."

"Sorry. I didn't know. So Mark caught you on the rebound?"

Ignoring the probe, she said, "I suppose after that I got lost for a while and by the time I found myself I was already committed to heading in this direction. What about you? Where did you hail from originally?"

"Neat about-face on the background information, Sarah." Ben grinned and she marveled again at the way his craggy features were transformed by that slightly lopsided smile.

He said, "I was born in San Diego. Thought I wanted to be a professional athlete when I grew up—got a football scholarship to San Diego State, but I really preferred surfing and I wasn't sure if there was a living in that. Then I wiped out while I was bodysurfing a killer wave at the Wedge and broke my back. The Newport Wedge is the ultimate challenge for bodysurfers—huge waves break in shallow water. I didn't tuck out in time."

"How awful," Sarah murmured. "But you made a remarkable recovery."

"It took over a year. While I was in the wheelchair my brother used to take me down to the beach. I got tired of watching the action and began sketching. One day a school of dolphin were playing in the bay and I did my first marine life. A tourist made me an offer for it before it was even finished."

"And the rest is history?"

"More or less. When I recovered I took up diving and underwater photography, so I could study the undersea world, and switched my major to marine biology." He squinted at her. "Cobalt blue."

"I beg your pardon?"

"Cobalt blue. That's what I'd use for your eyes. Your hair I'd have trouble with, trying to get the exact blending of sorrel and chestnut and terra-cotta, all burnished with tawny lights."

Sarah felt her color rising and concentrated on her coffee.

"Don't be embarrassed, Sarah. I'm an artist, remember? I see the world in color. I also appreciate great bone structure and wonder if it's possible to capture on canvas that blazing honesty that shines from your eyes." He paused. "I'm not coming on to you."

Looking up, she met his gaze. "Aren't you?"

He chuckled. "Well, maybe a little. But my motives are honorable. I make it a point to keep my flirting light with married ladies."

She was almost tempted to tell him what had transpired at the bank. It would be so good to share her doubts with him, but thinking about doing so made her feel disloyal to Mark.

"No change in your husband's condition, I take it?" Ben said, his voice turning somber.

She shook her head, finished her coffee and stood up. "I've got to go. Thanks for the coffee."

Ben accompanied her back to her rental car. Opening the door he said quietly, "I'd like to be your friend, Sarah. No ulterior motives, no pushing for more, I promise."

"I certainly seem to be in need of a friend, don't I?" she responded wistfully.

As she drove away she found herself thinking about the hotel fire. Her friends and her parents' friends, had rallied around her. She had no other family. Her parents had been well into middle age when she was born and none of their relatives had survived past Sarah's teen years.

The day after her parents' funeral she went to bed and stayed there, unable to find any reason to get up. Her fiancé, Alan Braithwaite, was buried by his grieving parents in Florida and Sarah didn't attend his funeral.

One by one all of her friends deserted her as her depression deepened and she refused to seek help. She still didn't recall much about the months between the funerals and the day she walked into Mark's office and asked for help, but somewhere along the way she became part of a class action suit filed on behalf of the victims of the fatal fire.

The lawsuit was still in progress, with the lawyers suing everybody—the hotel owners, the management, the makers of the smoke alarms and overhead sprinklers. Sarah hadn't wanted to think about any of it, so she signed some papers, she wasn't sure what, and put the legal maneuvering out of her mind.

There was a small insurance policy on her father, nothing on her mother, and they left her a modest estate, enough to live on during those lost months. When the money dwindled and she realized she had to go back to work she finally admitted to herself that she needed psychiatric help to overcome her depression.

Mark had gently coached her through the stages of denial and grief and acceptance, had helped her deal with her guilt, and taught her to live again. Was it any wonder that she fell in love with him? She had been so alone, so isolated.

Now here she was on the West Coast, feeling alone and isolated and yes, abandoned again.

She told herself that she must guard against allowing Ben Travis, neighbor, artist, handyman, mechanic, to assume too great a role in her life. That had been her mistake with Mark.

THAT EVENING SHE TOLD Harriet what happened at the bank and Harriet promised to wire her New York bank for money. She had only about fifty dollars in cash, which she gave to Sarah.

"I'm sure there's been some sort of mix-up," Harriet said. "I'll open an account here tomorrow."

Feeling depressed and now a little humiliated, Sarah unpacked her sewing machine and worked on the curtains for Emma's windows, then read her a story. Harriet had retired for the night by the time she finished.

A warm bath did little to relax Sarah. Lately, her dreams were filled with images of flames and smoke. Since the garage burned down, thoughts of fire so dominated her nights that she was reluctant to sleep.

Donning her warmest robe, she went downstairs to the captain's mess, taking Mark's manuscript with her. Perhaps when the room was all shipshape she'd be able to imagine Mark working in there. For a while she routed dust and cobwebs from the built-in cabinets and then unpacked file folders and stashed them away. But her gaze kept drifting to the manuscript folder lying on the desk. She was torn between wanting to read on and being fearful of what she might learn about her husband.

There was no doubt in her mind that Mark had intended to sort those papers and notes before passing them along for her to edit and put on the computer. Perhaps it would be wiser to let him select what she should read. Was she invading his privacy, as Harriet had accused? But the answer to so many questions about her husband might be right there, in his own words....

She sat down and opened the folder.

Since the contents had spilled when she first opened the packing crate, none of the pages were in order, and although some were numbered, many were not. She found herself reading passages without knowing the context.

Mark had switched between first and third person, giving the disturbing impression that when Mark spoke of "Matt Layton" he was attempting to disguise the fact that he was writing from experience, about real people.

...Matt knew he was becoming obsessed with Selma Johnson. With his other patients he found himself watching the clock, barely listening to them. He was impatient with their self-absorption, brusque with his comments. Selma was the first thing on his mind when he awoke in the morning, the last thing he envisioned before he fell asleep.

He could imagine each detail of her face—her eyes, her lovely alabaster skin.

For Selma's appointments Matt selected his clothes with care, often pressing his shirts even though the laundry had done an adequate job. He had his hair styled, shaved at lunchtime.

One day, on an impulse, he bought a dozen roses and put them in a vase on the desk.

Selma saw them immediately and gave him a knowing smile....

Sarah stared at the words. Alabaster skin. An image of Mae Peterson's pale complexion intruded momentarily. She blinked it away and read on.

Matt watched as Selma crossed the room to the couch. He was acutely aware of the fact that it was the first time she chose the couch over the chair.

Kicking off her shoes, she arranged herself on the couch, arms at her sides, one knee slightly raised. She wore a buttercup yellow minidress and it hiked up to her thigh. Matt pretended to read her file.

"How was your week?" he asked, eyes still fixed on the file notes but every nerve in his body focused on her.

"I almost called you the other night."

"You should have, if you needed to talk."

"It was past midnight."

"Any time you need to talk, please call. What happened? Did the nightmares come back?"

She nodded. "Worse than ever."

"Bryce?"

"It's not just the nightmares. I found out he's getting out of prison."

Matt felt an unpleasant jolt. "But you said he got seven years?"

Selma gave an inelegant snort. "He's served less than half his time. It's a joke. For killing a man, yes."

Matt remained silent.

She whispered, "What would you say if I told you I was there... when he did it. What would you say if I told you I helped him?"

Sarah had reached the end of the page and she turned it quickly, but the following page was out of sequence. She rifled through several more pages but couldn't find the continuation.

All the lights in the house suddenly went out.

Chapter Nine

Sarah stumbled through the unfamiliar house in the suffocating darkness, stubbing her toe, colliding with a wall, trying not to panic. Were there any flashlights or candles? Where were the fuse boxes? She felt her way to the kitchen, knowing there were matches in a drawer by the stove.

After burning her fingers a couple of times as she searched for a flashlight, she discarded the matches.

Get a grip, Sarah. A fuse has blown, that's all. It's the middle of the night. You can get it fixed tomorrow. It will be light in a few hours. Go to bed.

She managed to get up the stairs without crashing into anything. As she slipped into bed she said a quick prayer that neither Emma nor Harriet would awaken in the powerless house.

Within minutes, she began to sleep fretfully. The dreams came again. In one, flames were all around her but she could hear the distant wail of sirens and knew help was on the way.

No, not sirens, it was the phone. Sarah reached for it, nonsensically hoping it was Ben calling to comfort her, blinking in the fact that the luminous dial of her watch read 2:33. She had been asleep barely an hour.

"Sarah—hi, it's me. This couldn't wait for morning."

Mae Peterson. An immediate ache of tension centered itself between Sarah's eyes. At the same instant she wished she'd requested an unlisted phone number. "What is it, Mae?"

"You won't believe what I found out about your husband."

Sarah's heart skipped. "You've been to the hospital?"

"No, hon. I'm talking about what your old man was up to *before* his accident."

"I don't want to hear any gossip about my husband, Mae, especially not at two-thirty in the morning. Please mind your own business and leave me alone. If you don't, I'll be forced to get a restraining order."

"Hey, simmer down! I didn't realize what time it is. I had a late date. I just thought you should know that Dr. Mark had an interesting conversation with a boat owner down at the marina the day before you were due to arrive."

"I don't want to hear this—"

"He said his wife was going to come into a bunch of money when a big lawsuit was settled. He was looking to buy a yacht."

Sarah had been about to slam down the phone, but now she hesitated.

Mae's voice continued in a soft purr. "A big expensive seagoing yacht, hon. Did he ever talk to you about that? You can check with the owner of the *Pacific Dancer* if you don't believe me. You know, I've been thinking, maybe it was a blessing in disguise that he crashed over the cliff before you got here. Who knows what he planned to do with you after he got his hands on your money?"

Sarah hung up.

Shivering, she curled up beneath the bedcovers, castigating herself for allowing the woman to place doubts in her mind. Clearly, Mae Peterson had some motive for taunting her. Besides, why would Mark need her money? He was wealthy.

She thought of her visit to the bank that day. He had not transferred any funds there. The house on Long Island had not yet been sold. Mark had given up a lucrative practice, thus ending that income. He had enjoyed an opulent lifestyle. What if the Lasiters were not as rich as he had indicated? Had Mark been counting on her settlement to support them while he tried to make it as a novelist?

Sarah rejected the idea. He had never once questioned her about the lawsuit. Besides, it was liable to drag on for years.

She slept fitfully and awakened at dawn. Checking the bedside lamp, she found the power was still off. Dressing in a mohair sweater and jeans, she went outside to look for the fuse box. Flipping all the buttons in the box had no effect.

Back inside, she picked up the phone to call the electric company. The phone was dead. She scribbled a note for Harriet. *Power and phone out, gone to Ben's house to call.*

Ben answered his doorbell after the first ring. He was fully dressed.

"Sarah . . . good morning."

"Sorry to bother you so early, Ben. Is your power on?"

"Yes. Isn't yours?"

"No. My phone's out, too."

"I'll go back with you and take a look. If we need to call for a repairman, I've got a cellular phone in my car."

For the first time all night, Sarah suddenly felt relieved . . . and safe.

MUCH LATER THAT DAY, Sarah sat down at the kitchen table determined to talk honestly with Harriet. "Harriet, I'm wondering if you and Emma should go back to Long Island."

"What? But Mark can't be moved."

"No. I'll stay here with him. But I think perhaps it would be better for you and Emma to go home."

"Why? Are we a burden to you?"

"No, of course not. But I'm beginning to realize there was more to Mark coming out here than he told us. I'll be frank, Harriet. Something strange is going on here. The accidents, the garage fire, Mark's actions before we arrived. I just found out that there was no power failure last night, nor did the phone go out. It's no wonder Ben couldn't fix things. The electric company just told me that somebody may have deliberately sabotaged our power and cut our phone lines. Sarah started to mention Mae Peterson, but refrained. She didn't intend to frighten Harriet, just make her see reason. Besides, it was possible the strange woman meant no harm.

Harriet was staring at her uncomprehendingly.

"I believe we may be in danger," Sarah said. "I think you should take Emma home. Mark would want you to be safe. I'll stay here until he recovers."

"We can't go home," Harriet whispered.

"Why not?"

"We don't seem to have any money. I just had a call from my former bank manager. Mark closed all the accounts."

"You didn't have your own account?"

"Yes. But when Mark told me he wanted to move out here, he suggested I give him a power of attorney so he could handle all the financial matters."

Sarah gasped. "Are you telling me we have no money at all?"

Harriet spread her hands helplessly.

"Did your bank manager tell you where he had transferred the accounts?"

Harriet's voice was barely audible. "He said Mark took cash. All that's left is Emma's trust fund, but it can't be touched until she's eighteen."

"Portrait of a man on the run," Sarah murmured grimly.

"I don't understand any of this," Harriet said. "Whatever's happening, I'm sure there's a reasonable explanation." She paused. As if attempting to restore normalcy to their lives, she continued. "Our first mail delivery came today. I haven't opened anything. I put it all on the desk in the study."

Sarah barely heard her. She was making a mental inventory of their valuables and wondering where the nearest pawn shop was located. There didn't seem to be any other solution to their sudden poverty. They had to eat. Fingering her diamond engagement ring, she went into the captain's mess and sat down at the desk.

The incoming mail was all addressed to Mark. She picked up a letter opener with a brass sailing ship handle and slit open the first envelope. It contained a bill from the hospital for Mark's care in ICU and it was astronomical.

There were bills covering installation from the electric, gas, and phone companies. One from the Emerald Cove Water Company and another from the county for trash collection.

She almost didn't open the last envelope, which was clearly yet another bill, until the New Jersey return address caught her eye. Tearing open the envelope, she pulled out a statement of charges under the heading Meredith and Parker, Investigations. The items listed included several days' surveillance fees, database charges, and miscellaneous charges. A final report was being sent under separate cover.

Sarah stared at the statement. Her husband had hired private investigators to watch somebody. No name was given. The dates of the surveillance reports were spread over the three week period following their wedding, the last one dated the day they left for the West Coast.

There was no street address on the statement, merely a post office box number. But there was a phone number. Sara made a quick calculation. With the three-hour time difference it would be almost five on the East Coast. She wondered if the phone repairman was done yet and went outside to see. He was just finishing up. She could use her phone again.

An answering machine picked up her call on the first ring. "You've reached Meredith and Parker, Investigations. Leave your name, number and the date and time and we'll get back to you."

Sarah hesitated for a moment, then complied.

Something nagged at the back of her mind. Another call she'd intended to make. She remembered the phone number written on the napkin from Pasquale's Ristorante.

Passing the kitchen on her way upstairs to retrieve the napkin, she noticed that Harriet still sat at the table, staring out of the window. She looked so incredibly fragile.

No area code had been written on the napkin with the number, but she assumed it would be the New York area code.

Three thousand miles away a female voice with a peevish edge picked up the phone. "Yes?"

Sarah drew a deep breath. "I'm calling for Dr. Mark Lasiter."

There was a moment's hesitation. "So?"

"He's been in an accident."

"What do you expect me to do about it?"

"I . . . just thought you'd want to know."

The phone was slammed down in her ear. She stared at the receiver, picturing a beautiful dark-haired woman with voluptuous curves, and wondering if she'd just spoken to the alter ego of Mark's fictional Selma.

SARAH DECIDED they'd all feel better after a square meal and she certainly needed something to occupy her hands as she wrestled with the myriad problems facing her.

She had bought stewing beef, vegetables and noodles. While she chopped onions, floured and browned the beef, she considered her options. They were pathetically few. Time after time she thought of turning to Ben for help. But she knew she couldn't—especially in light of her attraction to the man. Mark hadn't been entirely honest, perhaps, but she was still his wife.

There had to be a way to find out where Mark had put his money and gain access to at least living expenses. Harriet would know the name of Mark's personal lawyer and accountant. First thing in the morning she would phone New York again and explain their predicament. As soon as they had some ready cash, she would send Harriet and Emma home to Long Island and she would move into the bed-and-breakfast inn. If Mark didn't come out of the coma soon, she would have to look for a job.

When the tempting aroma of beef stew filled the house she called upstairs to Harriet, who had gone to take a nap. "Dinner in ten minutes. Will you wake Emma now and come down to eat?"

Ten minutes later when she hadn't heard any movement upstairs, she went up to Harriet's room. The elderly woman was still sound asleep. Sarah decided not to wake her.

"What say we play a game of dominoes after we clear the dishes?" Sarah said brightly as Emma ate. "I found an old wooden set in the captain's mess."

"Don't know how."

"You know your numbers, don't you? It'll be easy. I'll show you."

Harriet slept all through the evening. Sarah put her dinner in the refrigerator, played dominoes with Emma for a while, put her to bed and, exhausted, went up to her own room.

She lay in bed feeling her aching muscles twitch and tried to remember what it had been like to curl up in Mark's arms before falling asleep, but all she could recall was waking up to find him gone.

THE PHONE RANG at seven the next morning. A male voice said, "Mrs. Lasiter? This is Dr. Conroy at the hospital. Could you come down here right away?"

Half-awake, Sarah mumbled, "Has there been a change in my husband's condition?"

"Yes. But I'd rather talk to you in person. How soon can you get here?"

"Forty-five minutes."

Fully awake now, Sarah threw on her clothes. She could hear Harriet moving around downstairs, and when she hurried down to the kitchen found that she had made coffee and toast.

"The hospital called. The doctor wants to talk to me." Sarah decided not to mention there'd been a change in Mark's condition, just in case it was a change for the worse. No need to worry his grandmother yet. If it proved to be good news, she could call from the hospital.

Harriet nodded. Her lips were compressed into a thin line and despite having slept for at least twelve hours, she looked haggard. Sarah massaged a frail shoulder reassuringly. "Everything's going to be all right. Don't worry."

Taking only a few minutes to drink some coffee, Sarah took a piece of toast to eat en route.

At the hospital she took the elevator up to ICU and told the nurse that Dr. Conroy had sent for her.

The nurse looked baffled. "Dr. Conroy? But he isn't in this morning. Are you sure he called?"

"I'm positive. He said there'd been a change in my husband's condition."

"I'm sorry, Mrs. Lasiter, but there's been some mistake. There's no change in your husband's condition and Dr. Conroy left for a medical conference in L.A."

"Somebody claiming to be Dr. Conroy called me," Sarah insisted.

The nurse picked up the phone. "I'll page Dr. Alvarez, he's in charge while Dr. Conroy is away. We'll get to the bottom of this."

It took almost an hour to check with all of the hospital staff but eventually Sarah accepted that the call had been a hoax. If it had been a woman who called she would have suspected Mae Peterson using a disguised voice. But the caller had definitely been a man.

"Perhaps you should report this to the police," Dr. Alvarez suggested.

"I don't know what they could do. I have no idea who called."

Sarah stayed at Mark's bedside for another hour, trying to think of something to say, wishing she had some good news to impart, wishing there were not so many troubling questions she needed him to answer. Did he hear her? Or was he forever lost to her? Had he, in fact, ever really been hers?

She thought of the woman in New York who had answered the phone and angrily hung up when she tried to tell her about Mark. Was she Selma? And what was Mae Peterson up to? What could a Realtor from Nevada possibly want from them?

Realizing that she hadn't had an opportunity to ask Harriet for the names of the Lasiters' lawyer and accountant, Sarah decided to return to Cliff House in order to call New York before the business day ended there.

The front door was slightly ajar. Sarah made a mental note to warn Harriet to keep it locked. The house seemed unnaturally quiet. She called, "Hi, I'm back—where is everybody?"

No response.

She went into the kitchen. A note was attached by a magnet to the refrigerator door.

Harriet's spidery handwriting was almost too faint to read. "Dear Sarah, Coming here was a mistake. I've decided to take Emma to stay with friends. Harriet."

Chapter Ten

Sarah reread the note several times, then went upstairs. There were clothes in both Harriet's and Emma's closets, but it was possible some items had been taken. Sarah sat on Emma's bed, Harriet's note in her hand, feeling overwhelming sadness.

Even though she had suggested to Harriet that they return to New York, she hadn't expected they would depart so abruptly and without saying goodbye.

She thought of the phony call from the hospital. Was it possible someone wanted to get her out of the way? Her heart began to pound against her ribs.

Reading the note again she decided that it had definitely been written by Harriet. But what if someone had forced her to write it? She could call the police, but would they believe her suspicions? How could she even prove Mae Peterson existed?

She ran into her own bedroom and grabbed the phone. There was only one taxi company in town. A call to the dispatcher established they had not sent a cab to Cliff House. She called the car rental agency. No, no one named Lasiter or fitting Harriet's description had rented a car.

How then had they traveled to the nearest airport or train

station, some twenty miles away? And where did Harriet get the money to travel?

Sarah prowled through the empty rooms, seeking some clue to their sudden flight, fighting a rising sense of panic. At length she went to the phone and dialed the number of Mark's former office in Manhattan. Perhaps the psychiatrist who had taken over the practice would be able to give her the number of Mark's lawyer.

The line was busy and before she could dial again the phone rang. She snatched up the receiver. "Hello."

"Mrs. Lasiter?" She didn't recognize the voice.

"Yes."

"This is Al Meredith."

Meredith. Of course, the investigator who had sent Mark a bill.

"Thank you for returning my call. Mr. Meredith, my husband was in an accident. He's in a coma. I need to know exactly why he hired you."

"I'm sorry, ma'am, but that's privileged information. Client confidentiality, you know."

"It seems to me that the safety of your client's wife and family should outweigh such considerations, especially since your client is now in a coma and there's some doubt about the cause of his accident. My husband's grandmother and daughter may have been kidnapped. I have reason to believe I am in danger."

"Okay, I guess under the circumstances you probably should be told... We were hired to watch *you,* Mrs. Lasiter."

BEN DID not question her when she appeared on his doorstep and if he noticed she was shivering and agitated he made no comment, patiently waiting for her to explain her unexpected visit. He brewed a pot of tea as she prowled nervously around his kitchen and living room. Then he poured the tea into a sturdy mug, added a generous amount of rum, cream, and a teaspoonful of sugar. "Guaranteed to warm you to your toes and cheer you up. It's an old English remedy of my grandmother's."

Sarah thanked him. Taking a sip, she felt the fiery warmth course through her body. Clutching the mug in both hands, she looked around. This was the first time she had been inside Ben's house. Like the man, it was rough-hewn and simple, the furniture plain but comfortable. Through a floor-to-ceiling window she could see a bronze sculpture of a dolphin, poised above a fountain, on a flagged patio. There was only one of his paintings, hanging over the fireplace in the main room of the A-frame.

Seeing her look around, Ben said, "No, my wife the interior decorator didn't do this place. I bought it after she died."

"How did you cope?" Sarah asked.

"Not very well at first. But they're right, it gets a little easier with time. You don't stop grieving, or missing the life you had together, but you fill up the hours with other things, other people. It took me a while to learn that. At first I isolated myself out here and worked day and night. Then I agreed to show up at some of the galleries exhibiting my work. I tried my hand at sculpting and got a few commissions, which meant traveling to the sites."

"You did the bronze dolphin on the fountain? I'm impressed. It's magnificent."

"Thanks. I was spending so much time traveling that I found an apartment in San Francisco for business convenience. But I still do most of my work here."

He put another log on the fire. The room was cozy and Sarah felt warm and safe. At length she perched on the edge of a chair near the fireplace.

"Are you hungry? I made chili for lunch. I've got plenty."

She attempted a grateful smile. "I can't stay long. Ben... Mark's grandmother and Emma are gone. I called the police but they think everything's on the level because Harriet left a note."

He listened silently as she told him all that had happened in the past twenty-four hours. She hadn't intended to tell him about the disappearance of the bank accounts, or about the disturbing phone calls to New York, but somehow his quiet presence and unspoken empathy drew it all out of her.

She concluded, "I finally got through to the psychiatrist who took over Mark's practice, but he couldn't tell me anything. He said his own lawyer handled everything, through a company that specializes in professional practice sales. He doesn't know—or at least claimed he didn't know—the name of anyone who could help me find out where Harriet might have taken Emma. I begged him to at least give me the names of some family friends, but he said he didn't really know Mark, except by professional reputation. He'd filled in for Mark occasionally in the past and originally they'd talked about a partnership. Then Mark abruptly asked if he would take over the entire practice."

Ben said, "You realize what all this adds up to, I suppose?"

"A man who wants to disappear? But, Ben, he wasn't running from us, he brought us out here with him."

"Well, not exactly. He came out alone and sent for you later."

Sarah stared into the leaping flames in the fireplace. "He was looking for a place to live." The explanation sounded lame, even to her, and she wanted to believe in her husband.

"What about the fact that he hired private detectives to watch you? Isn't that a bit unusual for somebody just married?"

Sarah had no comment. She was still reeling from that revelation and couldn't imagine why Mark had hired someone to spy on her.

Ben leaned forward, "How about the Peterson woman telling you that he was talking about buying the *Pacific Dancer*—which, by the way, *is* for sale. What about that? Had he told you you might be going on a voyage?"

Sarah shook her head. She had not confided to Ben that Mark had said he was expecting his wife to come into a large sum of money with which he intended to buy the yacht, nor had she told him that in fact she was now penniless. There was already more than enough information to cast doubt on Mark's motives for marrying her.

She said in a low voice, "You must think me an awful fool."

"I'm inclined to agree with Harriet's assessment of your relationship with Mark."

"She talked to you about us?" Sarah was shocked.

"Only to the extent that in her opinion you didn't know each other well enough to marry and she believed that both of you were attempting to recapture lost loves. Sarah, I became involved with a woman shortly after my wife died. I know how easy it is to fall into that trap. You want so desperately for the hurt to go away, to feel connected to somebody again, that you simply don't see that you're pinning your hopes on a dream of happiness that can't be achieved with the person you're latching on to."

"Harriet didn't approve of me," Sarah said. "She felt Mark was marrying beneath himself."

"There's still a lot of truth in her assessment, though, Sarah. You had brutal losses only a year ago. You haven't had time to recover from them yet."

Was confusion from those losses still clouding her mind? she wondered. Was that why she felt so frightened? Or why she wanted to turn to Ben? Maybe there was a reasonable explanation for all the strange things that had happened. "Ben, have you heard any more about the body they found? Have they identified the man?"

"Not as far as I know."

"I've been wondering about the man Mae Peterson said was hurt the night she came to our door. It could have been his body they found. I—I should have mentioned him to the police but they seem so ready to discount things. Even today..."

"You didn't tell them?" Ben looked surprised.

"I should have, but—well, I had so many other things on my mind and frankly I didn't want to have anything further to do with Mae Peterson. I certainly didn't want to give her any more reason to harass me."

Ben picked up a phone, punched in some numbers, and handed it to her. "Tell them now. In fact, tell them about all the Peterson incidents and mention that fake call from the hospital."

"Emerald Cove Police Department," a female voice responded.

Sarah identified herself and asked if the body of the man found down the cliff had been identified yet.

"Do you have some information regarding him, ma'am?"

Sarah began to relate how Mae Peterson had come to her door begging for help with an injured male companion.

"Mrs. Lasiter, hold on. We'd better have an officer come out and take a report. Are you at home?"

"Yes, or at least I will be in a few minutes."

Hanging up, Sarah said, "I have to go home. An officer is coming out to talk to me."

"I'll go with you," Ben said at once.

"No, I'd rather you didn't. I'm calm again now. I guess I panicked when Harriet took off without a word."

"I don't like the idea of you being alone in that house."

"I'll be all right. I really shouldn't have left. Harriet will probably call me when she arrives at wherever she's going. You didn't hear a car go up the hill, did you?"

He shook his head. "But I was in what I grandly call my studio, working on a new sculpture, and I had the radio on. Call me after you talk to the cops, okay?"

"MRS. LASITER? I'm Detective Elliot." He wore plain clothes and held up a badge. He was in his midthirties, tall and broad-shouldered, with reddish brown hair and a penetrating gaze.

Sarah removed the chain from the front door. "Come in. We can talk in the kitchen." She added apologetically, "I haven't got around to furnishing the living room yet."

"The kitchen's fine."

"Would you like some coffee?"

"No, thanks. You called about another accident a day or two after your husband's?"

She related what had happened the night Mae Peterson rang her doorbell.

Elliot asked, "Why didn't you tell the police officer who came to question you about this on the day the body was found?"

"I thought you probably already knew there'd been another accident. Miss Peterson said she was going to file a report."

His eyes, amber flecked with green, bored into her. She suddenly thought of a cat she'd once owned that used to look rather like that just before it pounced with claws unsheathed. "You knew a man's body had been found, and a couple of nights earlier you'd been told of an injured man in approximately that location. You didn't think it worth mentioning?"

She felt herself flush. "I...Detective Elliot, I've only been in California a few days, my husband is in a coma, I've had a garage fire, I've been trying to keep his elderly grandmother and four-year-old daughter from coming apart and...well, Mae Peterson proved to be somewhat of a pest."

As she started to relate the other incidents involving Mae, Sarah realized that her suspicions really did sound ridiculous. Mae had brought a coffee cake and flowers, telephoned a couple of times, had invited her to a café. Since Sarah didn't want to tell the detective about Mark's strange behavior prior to his accident, or mention his notes, she lapsed into embarrassed silence.

Elliot scribbled something in a notebook and she was glad that for an instant she was released from his unnerving stare.

When he looked up, he asked, "Do you know where Mae Peterson is staying?"

She shook her head.

"When she called you, did she give you a phone number?"

"No. There's something else—someone called me from the hospital pretending to be my husband's doctor."

"You think it was this Peterson woman?"

"No, but..." Sarah pressed her fist to the furrow between her brows, feeling a headache start.

His attitude changed slightly. "Probably a prank call. Some people read about accidents and make such calls. Who knows what sick pleasure they get out of it?"

Sarah wondered if she should mention Mae's strange actions at the fish market on the pier, or the hair-raising return drive to town, but decided against it. She would sound paranoid.

Paranoia is fed by unfounded fears that are, in a sense, normal, Mark had written in an article she prepared for publication for him. *The mammalian brain beneath the cerebral cortex that controls our primal urges is where—deep inside the limbic system—neurons, hormones and electric pulses create paranoia. In our evolutionary past we probably needed paranoia in order to survive, but like our appendix, it's no longer useful. Confused signals from our limbic system trigger unwarranted fear and panic, probably due to biologic stress.*

The detective was watching her with an odd expression on his chiseled features. "Anything else, Mrs. Lasiter?"

She thought of the power and phone being cut off, but decided against mentioning that, too. Somewhere at the back of her mind hovered the thought that she knew too little about Mark's activities. Perhaps it was wrong to want to protect her husband, but she didn't want the police to get the idea, as Ben Travis had, that Mark had been running from something.

"No. I just thought you should talk to Miss Peterson about her friend."

"I'll be in touch," Elliot said as she showed him to the door.

She watched him walk to his car, his gaze sweeping his surroundings, lingering on the gutted garage. He turned, one hand on the car door, and looked back at the house with that policeman's suspicious gaze. Sarah drew back inside, feeling guilty without knowing why.

The phone rang and she ran to grab it. "Harriet?"

"Why, no, Sarah. It's me, Mae."

Chapter Eleven

"What do you want, Mae?"

"You sound panicked, hon. You expecting a call from someone else? I could call back."

For an instant, Sarah felt as if she were going crazy. Mae sounded so normal, even concerned. Was she wrong in thinking the woman was up to no good? "Why did you call? I asked you to leave me alone."

"Yeah, I know. You're pretty upset by everything that's happened. I didn't take offense. Anyway, I called to tell you that I've rented a house in Emerald Cove and I'd like you to come over for lunch. I figured since you spend your mornings at the hospital anyway and we're only a couple of blocks from there . . . you could come straight here."

Sarah was speechless. Again, Mae made the invitation sound so reasonable.

"Come on, Sarah, it will take your mind off your troubles. Besides, there's somebody I want you to meet. After all, you were willing to brave a midnight storm to save him."

Sarah thought of her conversation with Detective Elliott. Why hadn't she kept her mouth shut? Maybe Mae was on the level, and stress was making Sarah's imagination work overtime. She asked, "The man who was with you the night you came to my house?"

"Uh-huh. He's back from Las Vegas. He wants to thank you."

"There's nothing to thank me for. Besides, you said he's a married man. I really don't want to meet him."

"He's married, hon." Mae laughed heartily. "He's also my brother."

She was still laughing when Sarah hung up the phone.

"SHE'S A PATHOLOGICAL liar," Sarah fumed. "She's trying to drive me crazy. What did Mark used to call it? *Gaslighting.*"

Ben put a steaming bowl of chili in front of her. "Gaslighting? Is your husband an old-movie buff? I am or I wouldn't have known what you meant."

Sarah looked at him in surprise. "It's from a film?"

"Charles Boyer tried to make...Ingrid Bergman, I believe it was, think she was going insane. I have a small collection of old films if you're interested."

She took a mouthful of the searing chili to avoid answering that in all probability Mark was old enough to have seen the film in a theater. It bothered her that she was beginning to engage in these tiny evasions whenever Ben brought up the subject of her husband.

"Right now I doubt I'll ever be able to take the time to see a film," she said at length.

They were in Ben's living room, eating from a low table in front of the fire. Ben had called and offered lunch again. She'd been glad to escape from Cliff House after Mae's call, and had convinced herself that Harriet wouldn't call until evening.

"Did you tell Mae you'd told the police about the accident?"

"No," Sarah said. After a long pause, she continued, "Your chili is delicious, by the way."

"It's one of only three culinary accomplishments I've mastered."

"And the other two are?"

"Welsh rarebit—not to be confused with rabbit—and shark tacos. You'll have to try them sometime."

He laughed at her carefully noncommittal expression, then piled another log on the fire. The flames licked and crackled. Warmth radiated from them. Watching Ben's muscles flex as he lifted the log, she had a fleeting vision of how comforting it might be to be held in those powerful arms.

To cover the traitorous thought, she asked quickly, "Is it always this cold and damp here? I know it's winter, but somehow I expected a less harsh climate in California."

"It's a far cry from southern Cal, I'll grant you that."

"But you prefer it up here?"

"I can work up here. Few distractions...well, at least until you came along. If I was still down south in all that endless sunshine I'd be tempted to hit the beach a mite too often."

"You're kidding."

"No, I'm not. Perfect weather and the soul of a bum are a bad combination when your livelihood depends on self-discipline. No time clock to punch, no boss breathing down my neck, clear skies and a good surf running...hell, I'd be gone."

Sarah smiled. "I find that hard to believe."

"Believe it. I allow myself a couple of weeks a year down south, usually in July when the ocean temperature is up and the storms moving up the Baja bring the big surf."

"You can still surf, even after breaking your back?"

"Sure." He grinned. "Very carefully, of course."

"I wonder if Mark will be able to drive a car again after what he's been through," Sarah mused.

Ben's expression underwent a subtle change. He seemed about to say something, changed his mind and instead murmured, "Maybe he won't remember any of the details of the accident."

They were silent for a few minutes. Tiny explosions occurred in the glowing embers of the fire and the logs hissed and spat. The wind moaned around the eaves.

At length Ben said, "You're worried that he'll be different in some way."

She drew a deep breath. "No. I'm worried that even if he isn't the same man I married that I won't notice. Oh, Ben, I can't seem to capture his image in my mind. All I can see is someone in the shadows." She began to shiver, despite the warmth.

Ben stood up and walked from the room. He returned a moment later with a shawl and draped it around her shoulders.

She fingered the soft wool and saw it was yellowing with age. "Did this belong to your wife?"

"No. It was my mother's. It was sort of a family joke. She decided to take up knitting and this was her only project. She must have worked on it, off and on, for years. You have to understand, my mother just wasn't the knitter type. She ran a surf shop—sold boards, wet suits, fins and so on, and would shut up shop and hit the surf herself whenever the urge struck her. When I was a kid, I thought everybody's mom could handle a board or bodysurf. When she died my brother couldn't bear to look at the shawl, because we'd seen her working on it for so long. So I kept it."

Sarah nestled into the warmth of the shawl and couldn't help thinking that although she and Ben had led vastly different lives separated by a continent, she already knew him more intimately than she knew her husband. Intimacy, after all, had nothing to do with sex.

Ben added in a self-depreciating tone, "I suppose your husband and his colleagues would say that shawl is my security blanket, but to me it's a memento of my childhood and a small lesson in living that's my mother's legacy. I can still see her doggedly putting it together, stitch by stitch, determined not to let it defeat her, though she was as awkward as a clam with those knitting needles."

"I wish I could have known her. She sounds like someone I'd like. What about your father, Ben? What does he do?"

He paused a fraction of a second before answering, "He's a retired cop." He cocked his head to one side, listening. "Somebody coming up the hill, fast."

They both went to the window overlooking the cliff road. A black-and-white patrol car sped past.

"They can only be going to your place," Ben said. "We'd better go see what they want."

"I'll go," Sarah said. "There's no need for you to come."

Ben didn't argue with her.

Moments later, she pulled into the driveway of Cliff House behind the patrol car. The officer was approaching the house cautiously and spun around when the rental car arrived.

"I'm Mrs. Lasiter," she called as she opened the car door. "Can I help you?"

The officer walked over to her. "You made a 911 call about a prowler."

"No, I didn't."

"The call was made from the phone at this address, it shows up on the Emergency screen. A woman saying she was Mrs. Lasiter told the dispatcher somebody was trying to break in. Is there another Mrs. Lasiter in the house?''

''No...unless my husband's grandmother is back.'' Sarah fished in her purse for her key as she ran to the front door.

But Harriet had not returned. The officer accompanied Sarah on a room by room search of the house.

SARAH CALLED BEN and told him it was a false alarm, then spent the rest of the day beside the phone, but Harriet didn't call. The house was unbearably quiet.

At midnight she gave up and went to bed. She had just fallen asleep when her doorbell rang. This time the patrol car's red light was flashing and two officers were approaching the house with guns drawn. They were less understanding than the first officer when Sarah insisted she had not called 911.

''Look ma'am, it's a misdemeanor to make a false emergency call. The call was made from this residence. We'll let it go this time, but two 911 calls in a day is more than a misdial. Besides, crying 'wolf' could get you a slow response in a real emergency.''

''Officer, I didn't make those calls. Somebody must have broken in and used my phone.''

''While you were in the house? Did you hear anything?''

''No, but—''

''Okay, we'll check your doors and windows.''

They went through the house room by room. She wondered what they thought about the sparse furnishings, but the only comment they made was to inform her there was no sign of forced entry.

''This afternoon when the other call was made, I wasn't even here. The officer saw me drive up.''

"Where were you fifteen minutes before he got the call?"

She said she'd been at Ben's, then, in a shocked tone continued, "It takes you fifteen minutes to respond to a 911 call?"

"If we're patrolling the Coast Highway. Longer if we're in town. You should have thought of that before moving into a house stuck way out here."

"Yes," Sarah said heavily. "I should have."

After they left she called the hospital and spoke to the night nurse. "Sorry to bother you, but I wasn't able to get in to see my husband today and I wondered if there's been any change."

"No change, Mrs. Lasiter, but I thought..."

"Yes?"

"I guess I was mistaken. I thought you were in earlier this evening."

"What makes you think that?" Sarah asked sharply.

"I thought I saw a woman with your hair color, wearing a blue jacket like the one you have, leaving the ICU wait-ing room when I came on duty."

"I don't have a blue jacket. I've practically lived in a brick red parka."

"I was sure you came in at least twice wearing a blue jacket. Guess I was mistaken."

"Do you have any other patients in ICU?"

"No. Just your husband."

"Did the woman visit my husband?"

"As I said, I was just coming on duty. She may have come out of the ICU waiting room. But only immediate family..."

"Yes, yes I know. Thank you. Good night."

Sarah checked the lock on the front door again, then went back to bed. She was wide awake, worrying about the woman the nurse had told her about, agonizing over the 911 calls.

Someone must have gained entry to the house. Harriet had the only other key. Could she have given the key to someone else? Surely not willingly.

Sarah shivered. She just wished the police would pursue this. But surely, Emma and Harriet were fine. If there was no call from them by morning, Sarah would file a missing person's report.

Sleep eluded her. After tossing and turning for a while she gave in to the urge to read more of Mark's notes. She took the folder back to bed and pulled a blanket around her shoulders.

Her heart began to hammer as she read.

Selma called just before five and said she had to come in; it was an emergency. I sent my assistant home.

I locked the office door after Selma arrived, explaining it would be safe, since we were probably alone in the building. That musky perfume of hers, barely discernable, wafted toward me as she passed by. She was wearing one of those sundresses with thin shoulder straps. Yellow. She wore a lot of yellow. High-heeled strappy sandals, her usual bare legs.

"You said there was an emergency," I began.

She turned without a word and came into my arms. I felt her hands in my hair as she pulled my face down to hers.

Then we were kissing. Her mouth was sweet and hot and cool all at the same time and somewhere in my mind a voice whispered that I had to stop, but my hands were already slipping the thin straps down from her shoulders....

Sarah had read enough. She flung the page from her as if it were about to sting her hand and pulled the blanket closer. Mark had had an affair with a patient. She was sure of it.

But surely that patient could not have been Mae Peterson? She supposed Mae was attractive in a washed-out sort of way, but she was not the sensual, raving beauty Mark had described.

After a moment, when her heart stopped pounding, Sarah picked up another page. It was instantly evident that some time had passed and "Matt's" relationship with "Selma" had been ongoing for months.

I was becoming ever more fearful of discovery. I knew I should break it off. Every meeting I swore I would, but I was a slave to my own dark side in her presence.

The crisis came when she arrived at the office, unannounced, and demanded to see me. Fortunately I'd just finished with a patient.

Here Mark had switched back to third person.

Selma walked over to Matt's desk and picked up the photograph of his wife and baby.

"I always wanted a kid, but Bryce made me have my tubes tied." Her fingernails were painted bloodred and she scraped them over the glass in the frame and muttered, "Damn, if we could get Bryce and your wife out of the picture, it would be perfect."

Matt saw then the jaws of the trap he'd set for himself.

The next page was out of sequence. Sarah lay back limply on her pillow. Harriet told her that Mark's wife had committed suicide. Was it possible that she had been murdered?

Something struck the bedroom window with a soft thud.

She jumped out of bed, heart racing again.

Pulling open the French doors she called, "Who's there?"

She saw then what had hit the window and fallen to the deck of the balcony.

Lying at her feet was Emma's beloved teddy bear with the pearl button eyes.

A scream was trapped in Sarah's throat. The child never let Mr. Buttons out of her sight. She would never have left without him, nor would Harriet have forgotten to take him.

Chapter Twelve

"Calm down," Ben said, "and tell me what happened."

Shivering and breathing raggedly, Sarah found herself encased in comforting arms. "But first," Ben added, "let's go inside."

Keeping his arm around her, he led her into his living room and eased her down on the couch. She was clutching Mr. Buttons to her heart. "Ben, I'm sorry to come to you at this time of night, but I think Emma has been kidnapped, maybe Harriet, too."

He dropped a log on the still-smoldering fire in the fireplace and wrapped his mother's shawl around her as she blurted out that Emma's teddy bear had been thrown at the bedroom window.

"Ben, she wouldn't have left without Mr. Buttons. Oh, and something else, around midnight someone made another emergency call from my phone. The police were understandably annoyed with me. Now if I call 911 again... But I've got to try. I just know something's happened. I should have called from the house. I don't know why I came here. I—"

"Sarah," Ben said gently. "Just calm down. We're going to call the police and get some help."

She realized then that Ben was fully dressed, despite the lateness of the hour.

He saw her gaze flicker over the plaid shirt, jeans and boots he wore. "I was working late," he offered by way of explanation. "I wasn't abroad in the night breaking into Cliff House."

"Oh, Ben, I'm getting suspicious of everybody. I'm sorry."

"Look, Sarah, why don't you stay here and call 911 and I'll drive up to Cliff House and look around."

"No! I mean, I'd rather go with you."

"Maybe that would be just as well. If this is a kidnapping there may be a ransom call."

"I didn't think of that. Let's hurry back."

He grabbed a jacket from the hall stand and slipped a flashlight into his pocket. "We'd better take both cars. Are you up to driving?"

She had the keys to the rental car in her hand and nodded.

The wind had risen, blowing away the marine layer and revealing a full moon.

Following Ben up the moonlit ribbon of the road, Sarah felt some of her panic subside. He inspired confidence and trust, and she told herself she had to stop manufacturing reasons to suspect his motives for helping her. Cliff House was a gaunt silhouette against the sky. Ben waited for Sarah to park, then walked with her to the house.

"I locked the door, but I didn't turn on any lights," Sarah said. "I felt so—exposed—with all the bare windows." She was fumbling with the door key.

Ben took the key from her and unlocked the door. "Is the light switch to the left or right?"

"Right."

Light flooded the entry hall and Ben said, "Make the call while I look around. Which window was the teddy bear thrown against?"

Sarah directed him up to her bedroom as she reached for the phone.

To her relief, the emergency dispatcher sounded polite and concerned. Perhaps there had been a change of shift. As Sarah related that she believed a four-year-old girl had been kidnapped, she could hear the woman on the other end of the line rapidly tapping computer keys. Sarah hoped there'd been a change of shift for the police officers, also.

Ben came down the stairs as Sarah finished making the call. "I presume you left the French doors to the balcony unlocked after you picked up the teddy bear?"

"How stupid of me!"

"You were upset. Anyway, apart from that door being unlocked, I can't see any sign of forced entry through any of the other doors or windows."

"That's what the police said when they were here earlier."

"Which means," Ben said slowly, "that somebody has a key."

She felt tears sting her eyes. "Oh, Ben, thank you for not telling me I'm crazy. Thank you for not turning me away when I came to your house in the middle of the night. If one good thing has come out of my trip out here, it's meeting you."

He moved closer and took her in his arms again, brushed her tears away gently with his thumb, and held her close. His embrace was comforting and conveyed to her without words a powerful message, *everything's going to be all right.*

The comfort of his touch was overwhelming. She wanted to weep with relief that someone believed in her. She nestled close, laying her head on his chest and feeling his warmth. She smelled the clean scent of soap on his skin and a faint hint of a painting medium, linseed oil perhaps, on his clothes, reminding her that he worked with his hands, creating beautiful things. Somehow it was important to her to cling to that thought and put aside a nagging worry that her husband's manipulation of the human mind, his own included, was at the root of all of their problems.

She murmured, "I haven't told you all of it. In addition to the 911 calls I didn't make, a nurse insisted I was at the hospital when I wasn't. And I can't help but feel Mae Peterson is somehow behind all of it, which sounds paranoid, I know."

"You've had a rough time, Sarah. But from now on, you're not going to have to face it alone."

Sarah could have stayed in his arms indefinitely, shielded from forces almost too evil to contemplate, but he added, "There is something I noticed upstairs. Come on, I'll show you."

They went up the curving staircase to the landing and Ben led her into Emma's bedroom. Switching on the light, he pointed to the ceiling.

"See that square in the corner? I think it may be a trapdoor."

Sarah could see what at first glance looked like cracks in the ceiling. She caught her breath. "Do you think that's how an intruder got in?"

"I won't know until I get up there and look. There's probably only a crawl space up there, with no outside access. Do you want to wait until the police get here to check it out?"

"No. I'd rather know now. Do you need a ladder? I'm not sure we have one. Everything burned in the garage fire."

"I think I can reach it from a chair."

Ben pulled over a chair and climbed onto it. Pushing with the palms of his hands, he dislodged the trapdoor, which folded back out of sight. He took the flashlight from his pocket, flipped it on and pointed it through the opening.

"There's an attic up here. It seems to extend over the entire house. Looks like it's crammed full of maritime relics left by Cap'n Vaughan. I'm going up to look around."

Ben hoisted himself into the attic. Sarah supposed his work as a sculptor had given him his powerful biceps and honed his coordination. He went aloft with the ease of an acrobat. She could hear him moving items in the attic, then the creak of his footsteps over her head. Minutes later his face appeared in the open trapdoor.

"There's no way to get in here from the outside that I can see, but I'll have another look in the daylight. Stand aside, Sarah, I want to drop something down."

A moment later a lethal-looking object clattered to the floor.

"It's a hand harpoon," Ben said. "The kind they used on U.S. whalers back in the nineteenth century, but I believe they were still used in some other countries until about twenty-five or thirty years ago. Maybe you should return it to Captain Vaughan to store somewhere where it can't be found by kids."

Sarah stared at the harpoon. It looked like a javelin or a barbed spear attached by a cord to a long shaft. The barbed head still looked razor sharp. Ben dropped down onto the chair and she saw that he held a cardboard shoe box. He handed it to her.

"You'd better take a look at this. It was right by the trapdoor, like somebody put it up there in a hurry. I kicked it when I went up and the lid came off."

Sarah lifted the lid. An envelope marked Vivian, and bearing the return address of Mark's New York office, lay atop stacks of hundred-dollar bills.

For a moment she stared in astonishment at the money. She was about to open the envelope when the doorbell rang, then someone pounded on the front door. Startled, Sarah's head jerked in the direction of the sound.

"The police are here," Ben said. "What do you want to do with that money?"

"I'm not sure I want to tell the police about it, not yet, until I see what's in the envelope."

Ben's eyes met her—and held a judgment. They seemed to ask if she still loved her husband after all that had been happening and if she still wanted to protect him. Why, those eyes seemed to say, won't you simply turn the whole matter over to the police?

The doorbell rang again, more urgently.

"Give it to me," Ben finally said, "I'll hide it. You go to the door."

Sarah didn't know if what she was doing was right—only that Ben would stand by her decision. What if someone wrongfully thought she could instantly come up with ransom money? Could she use the money in the shoe box?

Sarah was breathless when she opened the front door to one of the uniformed officers who had responded earlier.

"You reported a kidnapping?" His expression was carefully blank.

"Please, come in."

She led the way to the kitchen, but he refused to sit down. She told him quickly about Harriet and Emma leaving, then showed him Mr. Buttons.

"You say your husband's grandmother and the little girl were gone when you arrived home this morning. Why didn't you report this before, when we responded to your earlier 911 calls?"

"They weren't my calls," Sarah explained patiently. "Harriet left a note, telling me they were leaving. So I wasn't sure anything had happened. But I know Emma would never have left without her teddy bear. Besides, someone threw it against my window tonight, long after I found that note."

"Do you have the note, ma'am?"

She looked around, her heart pounding. She felt so incompetent! And Emma and Harriet could be in danger. She tried to remember where she put the note. "No—I mean, I do, but I can't remember where I put it."

"You say somebody tossed the stuffed animal at your window? Did you see anybody?"

She shook her head. "The fog had drifted in then and I couldn't see beyond the balcony. By the time I ran down the stairs and went outside there was plenty of time for somebody to get away."

"Did you hear a car?"

Sarah ran her hand distractedly through her hair. "No, I didn't."

"What time was this?"

"About—" she glanced at the kitchen clock "—fifteen, maybe twenty minutes ago."

The officer looked up from the notes he was taking, and Sarah knew what he was thinking. She said hastily, "If you're wondering why I waited so many minutes before calling, it's because I—"

"Mrs. Lasiter came down to my house," Ben spoke from the kitchen door, causing the officer to spin around defensively. He relaxed somewhat as he evidently recognized Ben, and muttered, "Evening, Mr. Travis."

Ben said, "I've been helping Mrs. Lasiter search the house, but there's no sign of either the child or Mrs. Lasiter senior."

"I'm going to call for backup to search the cliffs as much as we can in the dark," the officer said, causing Sarah to shiver.

"It would have been better to call us right away. In the case of a missing child a search is always instigated immediately. Do you mind if I begin a search of the house?"

"Please, go ahead. I'll help, too," Sarah's voice rose a notch. "I know I should have called sooner, but I was sure they were fine...."

"Have you checked cupboards and cabinets, trunks, suitcases, the washer and dryer? You'd be surprised the places a kid can find to hide in."

Ben asked, "When can we get a search-and-rescue team up here?"

"As soon as it's light." The officer was already opening cupboard doors. "No basement, right?"

"No, but there's an attic," Ben answered. "I've checked it out. There are some boxes up there, but I don't see how a child could get to a trapdoor in the ceiling."

The officer slammed the dishwasher shut and looked at Sarah again. "Ma'am, why don't you see if you can find that note you say your husband's grandmother left?"

His tone was suspicious. He doesn't believe me, Sarah thought. Her eyes met Ben's in a silent appeal.

Ben said, "Maybe you left it up in your room."

Sarah escaped gratefully.

Running up the stairs, she wondered where Ben had hidden the box of money and wished she could read Mark's letter. Had she been wrong not to tell the officer about it right away? Some sixth sense warned that she should read the letter first.

Trying to recall what she had done with Harriet's note, Sarah remembered she had found it attached to the refrigerator door by a magnet. Since it was no longer there, perhaps she put it into her pocket. She went to the bathroom and fished out of the clothes hamper the shirt she had been wearing that morning. The note wasn't there.

Downstairs, the doorbell rang again.

Seconds later Ben came into the room. "Detective Elliot is here to talk to you."

"Where did you put the box?" Sarah whispered.

"Under your mattress—minus the letter, which I have here." He patted his jacket pocket. "If they find the money they'll just think Mark didn't believe in banks, which evidently he didn't. I'll give you the letter as soon as we're alone. Better go downstairs and talk to Elliot now."

Sometime later, feeling exhausted after being questioned intensively by the detective, Sarah was grateful when Ben said, "Mrs. Lasiter needs to rest now. She's told you all she knows. You've kept her up half the night. You've checked every nook and cranny in the house, so how about letting her lie down?"

Elliot said reluctantly, "Okay. We'll be outside waiting for the search-and-rescue team. I want to know right away if you get a phone call."

"Aren't you going to put a tap on the line?" Ben asked.

Elliot's disconcertingly opaque eyes rested briefly on Sarah. "Not until we're convinced this is a kidnapping. There's been no ransom call yet. Besides, the child is apparently in the custody of her father's grandmother, a blood relative."

Whereas I'm just the recently acquired stepmother, Sarah thought, with no rights at all.

The moment they were alone, Sarah exclaimed, "Ben, he thinks I've done something to Harriet and Emma!"

"No, he doesn't. He's just doing his job. Here, read your husband's letter. Maybe there'll be a hint in it about what's going on."

He pulled the letter from his pocket and handed it to her.

The brief note, in Mark's distinctive script, read: This is it, Vivian. If you come near me again I'll tell the police everything.

Chapter Thirteen

"Looks like blackmail money to me," Ben said grimly. "Who is Vivian?"

Sarah shook her head. "I don't know. I don't remember a Vivian. Not even as one of Mark's patients, at least, not while I was working for him."

"Go lie down. I'll call you if there's any news. Maybe after you've rested you'll recall the name."

In her room, Sarah kicked off her shoes and lay on the bed. Despite the fears and questions hammering her brain, she fell into an exhausted sleep almost immediately.

She awakened to the sound of helicopter rotors beating along the cliff and daylight spilling into the room. As memory rushed back, she cried out, "Emma—"

A warm hand instantly touched her cheek, then smoothed her hair from her brow. Ben stood beside the bed, holding a glass of orange juice.

"I came up to tell you the search-and-rescue team is here, combing every crevice and cave."

"Thank you." Sarah sat up and accepted the orange juice gratefully.

Ben said, "The tide will be turning soon and start coming in . . ." He broke off. "Sorry, Sarah, but it's a possibility we have to face."

She took a sip of juice. "Are the police still in the house?"

"Elliot and the patrolman are outside watching the search-and-rescue team. I wouldn't have come up to your bedroom if they'd been watching. Sarah..."

"Yes?"

"I get the feeling the cops don't think this is a kidnapping. They're searching for bodies."

"Oh, dear God!" Sarah buried her face in her hands.

Ben's hand rested reassuringly on her shoulder. "They asked me a lot of questions about how you got along with Harriet and Emma—and if you seemed to be on the verge of a breakdown because of your husband's accident. I told them you were the most caring and devoted stepmother I'd ever met and were holding up fine under the circumstances, but you're naturally frantic about Emma disappearing."

"I can't believe they'd suspect me. Oh, where could Harriet and Emma be? I was so sure nothing had happened to them. Ben, I've got to find them."

"Do you think you should tell the police about the money and the note to Vivian? This mysterious Vivian could have had something to do with Emma and Harriet's disappearance. You haven't remembered anything about her, have you?"

"No, I'm positive Mark never mentioned anyone named Vivian." Sarah paused, thinking that if her husband had been having an affair he would hardly have mentioned the name of his paramour.

She said, "If only Mark would come out of his coma! Ben, he cleaned out our checking and savings accounts, that has to be where that money came from. I don't know if I should tell the police about it or not. If Mark was being blackmailed, he must have had something to hide. I'm so afraid I'll uncover something that might ruin his professional reputation." *And his relationship with his daughter and me.*

"Well, it's up to you. As I told you, my father is an excop and one of his main complaints when he was with the San Diego P.D. was that people withheld crucial information that could have helped his investigations."

Sarah thought of the incriminating notes she had read, of the possibility that Mark had committed the ultimate malpractice by having sexual relations with a patient. She simply couldn't open up that awful possibility to police scrutiny—not yet, anyway. Of course, if it was true... well she couldn't bear to think of the implications of that now. She had to talk to Mark first and get the whole story. She said, "I must take a shower. I don't feel quite human."

Ben stood up. "I'll go downstairs and make some coffee." At the door he paused and looked back at her. "Then maybe I'd better get out of here. The cops are beginning to look at me sideways and I don't want to give them the impression I'm anything more than a concerned neighbor— even though..."

His eyes met hers. "Even though I'd like to be more, Sarah."

A tear formed and slipped down Sarah's cheek. "Oh, Ben, if only we could have met long ago, before—"

The morning silence was broken by the sound of vehicles starting up and Ben jerked his head in the direction of the roar of engines. "Sounds like the cops are leaving."

Sarah jumped from the bed. Both she and Ben ran down the stairs and reached the front door in time to see the search-and-rescue vehicles and a patrol car go roaring down the hill. Detective Elliot was sitting at the wheel of his unmarked car, speaking into his cell phone.

Ben ran across the driveway and had a brief conversation with Elliot. A moment later he returned to Sarah. "All he'd tell me is that there's a possible lead. He's going back to town. He said they'll let us know as soon as there's any news."

"Oh, thank God!" Sarah breathed. "What was it?"

"He wouldn't say yet. Go take your shower. I'll make the coffee."

THEY HAD SCRAMBLED EGGS and toast prepared by Ben, did the dishes, hovered near the silent phone.

At length Ben said reluctantly, "I'd better go home, in case the police come back. I don't want to cause any gossip about you. Call me when you hear, okay?"

Sarah nodded.

Ben hesitated. "Is there anything I can do for you? Anything at all, Sarah, just ask."

"I should call the hospital, see how Mark is, but I don't want to tie up the phone. Could you call for me?"

"Sure. Actually, I have to go into town this morning. I could stop by the hospital, if you like."

"Yes, I'd appreciate that."

"If there's no change in his condition, I won't call, so you can keep the line clear."

"Yes. That's a good idea."

"Will you be all right?"

"Yes, I'm fine."

Before leaving, Ben leaned forward and brushed his lips against her forehead. "Don't give up hope."

Sarah stood still for a moment, feeling the imprint of his mouth and wishing propriety had not decreed that he leave.

Then she sat down, looked at the phone, and willed it to ring with good news, about Mark, or Emma and Harriet.

The minutes, then hours, dragged by interminably.

By midafternoon black storm clouds gathered and there was a hard dark line along the horizon. She had to turn on the lights. The telephone remained stubbornly silent.

She stared at Mark's cryptic note, wondering if "Vivian" was the real name of his fictional "Selma." The thought surfaced that if Vivian had been expecting a blackmail payoff and didn't get it because Mark's car crashed, then she could have kidnapped Harriet and Emma in order to extort the money she knew Mark had available. But why hadn't she made a ransom call? And why had Mark himself refrained from calling the police? If Sarah called now, would she be unwittingly putting Emma and Harriet in danger?

Fearing the note might fall into police hands before she was ready to divulge her suspicions, Sarah took it into the captain's mess. If she slipped it in with the notes for his novel it would appear to be a part of the manuscript. She placed the note on the desk, weighted down by the ship in the bottle, as she opened the desk drawer to get the files.

Opening the folder, she paused, a quick vision of Mark's broken and bandaged body hooked up to the life support system, flashing into her mind. Hours had now gone by since Ben went to the hospital to inquire about him. What if Mark had come out of his coma in the meantime?

Her nerves on edge, she decided she would risk tying up the line briefly in order to call the ICU.

The day shift nurse paused before answering, somewhat stiffly, "No change in the last half hour, Mrs. Lasiter."

"Did Ben Travis come in? Did you talk to him?"

A note of bafflement crept into the nurse's voice. "Ben Travis?"

"Yes, you know, he's the local artist who did all those wonderful marine paintings in the lobby."

"I know who he is."

The following silence was ominous. Sarah said uncertainly, "Well, thank you. Please call me if there's any change."

It was only after she hung up that the nurse's comment registered. "No change in the last half hour," she'd said. What had she meant by that? Perhaps Ben had stopped by half an hour ago?

All at once, Sarah was acutely aware of the house surrounding her, closing in on her. The odd circular structure felt like a carousel conjured in a dream and she half expected it to start slowly revolving. Outside the wind demons hissed and whined around the cliffs and the sea uttered long mournful sighs. The house seemed bereft of purpose, a feeble imitation of the lighthouse it had replaced.

Feeling claustrophobic, Sarah opened the French windows. Instantly the damp wind claimed the room, sending pages from the file, bills and envelopes skittering from the desk. Only Mark's note to Vivian, safely anchored, stayed in place.

Gathering up the spilled items, she pushed them into a drawer. The bills reminded her of the box filled with money and she went back upstairs and lifted the mattress on her bed. The shoe box was still there. Was she wrong to say nothing to the police? Probably, but what if she needed the money to pay a ransom or to save Emma and Harriet?

Sitting cross-legged on the floor, she started to count the money. There was more than ten thousand dollars. She would have to take it to the bank at the first opportunity. But what to do with it in the meantime?

She found a large silk scarf, wrapped it around the bills, then stuffed the bundle into her roomiest shoulder bag. She dropped her wallet, address book, comb and lipstick on top of the money. Until it was safe in the bank, she would simply carry it with her.

Remembering then that the antique harpoon was still lying on the floor in Emma's room, she went to remove the loathesome weapon.

Again the dilemma of what to do with it. She'd return it to Captain Vaughan as soon as possible...but in the meantime? Unable to think of anywhere else, she took the harpoon to the captain's mess and put it into a long box that seemed to be some sort of sea chest. She stared at it with distaste for a moment, wondering how many majestic whales the simple yet lethal weapon had killed. The flat triangular head, sharpened at both edges and designed to pierce the tough skin of the great mammals, could surely rip human skin to shreds if improperly handled. Definitely not something she wanted a child to find.

The mere thought of Emma made her feel panicky, but she told herself to keep moving. She piled books on top of the chest in order to keep prying little fingers from lifting the lid until she had the chance to dispose of the weapon inside.

The house was growing colder and she went to the hall closet to get her parka. Surely at any moment she would be called to go and pick up Harriet and Emma.

She was about to close the closet door when she noticed that one of Mark's suitcases had been shoved into a corner, almost hidden behind his raincoat. Was it packed, ready for flight? She replaced her parka, pulled the suitcase out of the closet and snapped it open.

Beneath a couple of sweaters and several pairs of socks was a bulky manila envelope, marked Personal and Confidential. She unfastened the clasp and several letter-size lilac-colored envelopes addressed in green ink spilled out. They had been sent to Mark at his New York office. Her heart started to thump painfully as she withdrew a letter written in the same green ink.

Hey, lover,
Where were you last night? I told you your wife isn't going to keep your baby from you, didn't I? Viv is going to take care of everything. We're going to be a family, lover, never doubt it. So quit worrying.

Sarah picked up another letter, hoping it would offer some clue as to the present whereabouts of this woman. But it was more of the same. Vivian had to be the woman described in his notes. A patient. He had had an affair with her and she was now blackmailing him. There was no other explanation.

Could Vivian-Selma be Mae Peterson? Somehow the Nevada real estate agent didn't quite measure up as a femme fatale, but beauty and desirability were, of course, in the eye of the beholder. But the fact that the Nevada broker had confirmed that Mae had been one of their long-time agents presented a problem. New York was a long way from Las Vegas. It was difficult to conduct an affair at a distance of over two thousand miles.

The telephone rang shrilly and Sarah grabbed the extension phone beside her bed.

"Mrs. Lasiter, this is Detective Elliot."

"Have you found them? Are they all right?"

"No, we haven't. We'd like you to come down to the station. Can you leave right away?"

"The station? But why?"

"We'll explain when you get here."

"But what if someone calls me here?"

"Don't worry, they'll call back."

The line went dead before she could question him further.

A cold feeling of dread gripped her. Had they found bodies? Did they want her to go to the morgue to identify them? What other reason would they have to want her in town? And what if Emma and Harriet were fine? If she told Detective Elliot about Vivian, would she be endangering them?

How she wished Ben was with her.

At the hall closet she was about to grab her parka, then hesitated. She had worn the parka so frequently lately, because it was both warm and waterproof, that it was beginning to look a little grungy. She selected the full-length cashmere coat Mark had given her in New York.

Her hands shook as she picked up the car keys.

Chapter Fourteen

The Emerald Cove Police Department was housed in a nondescript brick building between the public library and post office. There were several patrol cars parked in front, but as Sarah hurried inside it occurred to her that this was a small town, with a small force of police officers, and probably limited resources.

The sergeant at the desk directed her to an open area where half a dozen desks, with computers and telephones, were being used by both uniformed and plainclothes officers.

Her hopes sank when she saw no sign of Emma or Harriet.

Detective Elliot rose to his feet as she approached his desk, his expression unreadable.

"Have you found them? Please, tell me," Sarah said.

"Sit down, please, Mrs. Lasiter." He indicated the chair next to his desk.

"Oh, God! They're dead, aren't they?"

"Why do you assume that?" he asked sharply.

Sarah wanted to pound on his chest. She swallowed. "Please tell me why I'm here. You told my neighbor you had a lead."

"We had a call informing us that the bodies of an older woman and little girl were lying under the pier."

For an instant the detective's face swam out of focus. Sarah's hand flew to her mouth. "Is it..."

"The call was apparently a hoax."

All of the breath drained from Sarah. She gripped the edge of the desk. No longer pondering the disloyalty to her husband, she wished with all her heart that Ben was at her side. She suddenly realized that a number of officers knew Emma and Harriet had left Cliff House. It seemed unlikely that one of them would have called the detective. "Who would do such a cruel thing?

"The call was made from a pay phone near the pier."

"Was it a woman who called?"

"Do you believe it was your husband's grandmother? Would she have reason to do something like this? What kind of terms were you on with her, Mrs. Lasiter?"

"Harriet would never do something like this. Never," Sarah declared, trying to keep the anger from her voice. "And we were on excellent terms, detective."

"But you immediately assumed a woman called. I didn't tell you it was a woman who called."

"The woman named Mae Peterson I told you about— when you came to question me about the man's body that was found... I thought she might have made that horrible prank call."

"This is the real estate agent who brought you cake and flowers and attempted to befriend you?" Elliot asked sarcastically.

"Why did you drag me into town to tell me you're no closer to finding Emma and Harriet? I could be missing a call!"

"I'd like to go over your statement again."

"My statement? You made it sound as if I'm under arrest."

"Not at all, Mrs. Lasiter, I just want to be sure I have all the facts straight."

Her head began to throb. She felt intimidated by the surroundings, the humming computer and uniforms and holsters bulging with guns. Not to mention by Elliot's unblinking stare.

"Now," he went on, "let's go back to when you first realized your stepdaughter and husband's grandmother were missing. Was there any kind of disagreement between you before that?"

THE NIGHT NURSE had come on duty at ICU and she pressed the door release. As Sarah entered, she saw at once that all of the open-sided alcoves surrounding the nurse's station were now occupied by patients. Nurses hurried from one to the next, busy hooking up IVs and respirators.

"Looks like you have a full house," Sarah remarked to the nurse at the station. "What happened?"

"A truck crammed full of migrant workers heading for the San Joaquin Valley collided with a van full of college students just north of here. We barely had enough beds. A lot of injured people came in."

Nodding sympathetically, Sarah went to Mark's bedside. She stared at her husband. What sort of nightmare did you drag me into, Mark? she asked silently.

She touched his hand, trying to recapture, in her mind at least, the man she had married. But all she could think of were the letters from Vivian, the wild fantasies Mark had apparently had about a patient, and about Emma and Harriet's disappearance. In light of it all, maybe she needn't feel quite so guilty for her growing attraction to Ben.

After a moment, she bent and kissed Mark's hand lightly and walked toward the exit.

"Leaving already?" the nurse called after her.

"Yes," Sarah said shortly, too weary to think up an excuse for the brief visit. She certainly couldn't tell the nurse she had to hurry home just in case she received a ransom call.

It was pitch dark by the time she reached Cliff House but she was able to discern the shadowy outline of a car parked in front. Ben, she thought gratefully.

Pulling into the driveway behind the other car, Sarah opened her door and was about to step out when Mae Peterson's voice hailed her. "Hi, Sarah. How are you doing?"

Sarah's knees felt unsteady as she climbed out of the rental car. *Keep calm.* "Good evening, Mae. I'm afraid I'm not in the mood for company."

"Trouble, hon? Hey, that's too bad. Your husband didn't make it, huh?"

"My husband's condition hasn't changed."

"Well, I thought you might need some company. It's pretty lonely up here, and I heard that the husband's grandmother and little girl left."

Sarah's chill deepened. "Where did you hear that?"

"Oh, I dunno. In town, I guess. I forget where."

"Please excuse me, I have a lot to do. I can't invite you to come in."

"Well, I'd really like to see the rest of your house sometime. Some weird place, huh? You know, me being in the real estate business and all, I'm interested in looking over possible listings. You might want to put it back on the market."

"Perhaps some other time."

"Sure, hon," Mae said. "I'll call you. Meantime, I brought you some saltwater taffy—got it at a place down the coast." She thrust a paper bag into Sarah's unwilling hands.

"Thank you, but I don't care for candy."

"Well, maybe the little girl will like it." Mae's voice carried an unpleasant undercurrent, as if she were daring Sarah to admit that Emma was missing.

Sarah felt her entire body tense. At least it seemed clear now that Mae hadn't kidnapped Emma and Harriet. If she had she would have made some demand, probably by phone. She never would have come here. As disturbing as the woman was, Sarah felt a vague sense of relief. Taking the bag of candy, she said, "Thank you. Good night."

Sarah started toward the house, hoping Mae wouldn't follow.

She reached the front door and inserted the key, expecting at any second Mae would appear beside her and demand entry. But Mae was still out there somewhere in the darkness. Now Sarah saw that headlight beams were slicing up the hill, and she let out a sigh of relief. The police or Ben must be returning. A second later Mae's car door slammed and the engine started.

Sarah stepped inside the house, closed the door and locked it. She was shaking.

She went to the kitchen and switched on the light, receiving her second shock. The room had been ransacked.

All of the cabinet doors were open, the contents scattered across counters and floor. The drawers had been pulled out. Everything had been dumped—cutlery, towels, kitchen utensils, paper goods. Even the refrigerator door yawned open. An open carton of spilled milk and a sticky mess of jam from a broken jar were on the floor.

For a second Sarah stared, disbelieving. Then she hurried through the house, turning on lights as she went. Every room was in the same state of disarray, even Emma's.

She felt a sharp pain in her side, and realized she was panting. Her shoulder bag was a comforting weight against her side and she clutched it tightly. *Mae Peterson's been inside this house, searching. She knows there's money here and she wants it.* She had to be Vivian, in spite of the distance between New York and Las Vegas. There was no other explanation. The police might never believe her, but Sarah was certain of it.

The doorbell rang and she heard Ben's voice. "Sarah, it's me. Are you all right?"

She picked her way through the debris to the front door. One look at her face told him something was terribly wrong and he put his arms protectively around her. "You're white as a ghost. What happened? A car passed me and it wasn't the cops. I thought I'd better check on you."

"It was Mae Peterson. Ben, come and look."

She led the way to the trashed kitchen. "The whole house is like this. Well, I haven't checked the captain's mess yet, but the rest of the house is."

"You'd better call the police."

Sarah ran her hand through her hair. "If I do, I'll have to tell them about the money and Mark's note. I feel . . . If I make a wrong move, I feel as if I might endanger Emma and Harriet."

"Where's the money?"

She patted her shoulder bag. "I took it with me. Detective Elliot called and said I had to go into the station." She told him of her interview and subsequent visit to the hospital. "Mae was here, waiting, when I got back. I'm sure she was the one who searched the house. But I have no proof. . . ."

"What's her motive for harassing you like this?"

"I have a theory—but I can't make all of the pieces fit."

"One thing's for sure, you can't stay here alone, Sarah. In fact, if the rest of the house looks like this, I'd recommend you simply close it up and come down to my place, and the hell with gossip."

Sarah had started to tremble again and he pulled her close and held her.

"Ben, as much as I want to go with you, I can't drag you into this nightmare. You mustn't get involved with me."

"Too late, Sarah. I care about what happens to you. I care about you."

"No! Don't say that. I'm some sort of female jinx. My fiancé died a horrible fiery death, my husband is in a coma from another terrible accident. I couldn't bear it if something happened to you, too."

"Nothing's going to happen to me."

"Aren't you listening to me? I'm more than bad luck to the men who care about me—I'm the proverbial black widow."

"You're tired, stressed out, Sarah. You'll feel better after a good night's sleep, but you're not going to get one here."

"But what if somebody calls?"

"Do you have an answering machine?"

She shook her head. "I didn't unpack one. Mark mustn't have wanted one here."

"We'll go down to my place and get one. I have a spare."

"No, Ben, I can't leave. What if Harriet and Emma are found? What if they're not really missing but simply come back? The police might need to talk to me...or the hospital might call."

"Okay, I'll stay here with you. No arguments. I'll sleep down here. But first I'll help you clean up your bedroom. You sure you don't want to report this?"

"Yes, I'm sure. What can I tell the police? Mae Peterson was here, she brought me some saltwater taffy and broke into my house and ransacked it? It sounds crazy. Detective Elliot doesn't believe me as it is. How do you think she got in?"

"With a key, as we suspected. Cap'n Vaughan was desperate to unload this place and he passed out keys to anybody who asked to see it. He should have told your husband to change the locks. We'll have them changed tomorrow."

"I'd better see what she did in the captain's mess."

"Appropriate name," Ben murmured as he followed her.

There were papers and books everywhere. The sea chest containing the harpoon was open, but the weapon was still inside, undisturbed. Everything from the desk was in a heap on the floor. The ship in the bottle was smashed on the surface of the desk and Sarah began to pick up the shards and drop them into the wastebasket.

She stiffened, pricking her finger on the broken glass as she remembered placing Mark's note under the bottle, then later putting it in with the notes for his novel. Dropping to her knees, she began to scrabble among the spilled papers on the floor.

"What is it, Sarah?" Ben asked. "What are you looking for?"

But she was on her feet, running to the hall closet. Ben caught up with her as she opened Mark's suitcase. "Sarah, what's missing?"

A long sigh shuddered away from her. "All of Mark's notes for the novel he was writing, and some letters I found

just today, from Vivian. Ben, I haven't told you what I
suspect Mark was being blackmailed about...I think I'd
better tell you everything and then you can decide whether
or not to stay.''

Chapter Fifteen

They worked side by side, picking up overturned furniture, sweeping up broken dishes, mopping spills. As they restored order to the kitchen, Sarah told Ben about Mark's notes and what she suspected, concluding, "I'm telling you all of this in confidence, Ben, because I trust you to keep it to yourself. You see, I don't know what was real and what was imagined."

"The letters you found were real. They seem to confirm your suspicions that your husband was romantically involved with someone named Vivian, too. Did you notice any dates on her letters to him?"

"No. But she mentioned Mark's first wife and his baby. She said she was going to take care of everything and they'd be a family, so the implication is that he was having the affair while married to his first wife. According to Harriet, she committed suicide but..."

Sarah hesitated to give voice to the thought. It was too monstrous.

"You're wondering if Vivian killed Mark's first wife?"

Sarah nodded. "She died of carbon monoxide poisoning... in her car."

"So she could have been unconscious and then put inside the car. Was there a suicide note?"

"Harriet didn't say. I didn't want to question her too much, because Mark had never told me about his first wife's suicide."

Ben's eyebrows raised in surprise, seemingly at the discovery that Mark would have kept that from Sarah. "Do you know of anyone named Vivian in Mark's life?"

Sarah shook her head. "After his first wife died, Mark's grandmother moved in with them to take care of Emma. There was no other woman in Mark's life until I came along. After his wife died, he must have broken off the affair with Vivian. Perhaps he suspected Vivian had killed his wife."

"I don't know your husband, Sarah, but... is there any possibility he might have been a coconspirator? Or at least had some knowledge of a crime? His note said he would tell the police everything."

"No! Absolutely not. Mark was—*is*—a kind, gentle man. That's why I keep searching for rational explanations." But she wasn't nearly as certain as she pretended to be. She recalled how Mark's notes had indicated that he was fascinated by the duality of the human mind, the dark side, and how he had wondered if it should be suppressed, or allowed to coexist in the human psyche. What if the violent psychosexual history of his imaginary patient had actually come from his own dark thoughts and desires? Could he have carefully concealed aberrant behavior from his friends, family, colleages ... from his wife?

"So where was the mysterious Vivian for—how long? Three years?" Ben mused.

"I have no idea. But that money and Mark's note indicate she came back into his life, don't they? Maybe he withdrew the cash to give to her, but didn't get a chance before his car went off the road. And where does Mae Peterson fit in? Maybe she knew Vivian and decided to blackmail Mark, or..."

"Or Vivian went to Las Vegas, changed her name to Mae and lay low for three years." Ben frowned. "But that seems unlikely if she had blackmail on her mind. Why wait that long before making demands?"

Sarah sighed. "I wish I knew how much of Mark's notes were from a case file and how much was imagined, or put together piecemeal from a variety of other cases. And I wish I knew how I'll be able to prove all of this to the police now that the notes are missing."

"What do you recall from Mark's outline for his novel? Any clues that might help us figure this out?"

"In the novel, the psychiatrist's patient says her boyfriend was convicted of murder, and hints that she was present when it happened. Ben, if Vivian is the model for that fictional patient and if she killed Mark's first wife... *what if she now has Emma and Harriet?*"

"Don't go down that road, Sarah, let's stick with the facts. You still don't know for sure that Harriet didn't decide to take off with the child. She left you a note, after all."

"Yes, but Vivian could have forced her to write it. Vivian has to be Mae Peterson, and Mark's fictional Selma. I can't figure out the how or why of any of it, but I know it in my bones."

The phone rang and Sarah jumped. Ben put his hand on her arm. "Steady."

He picked up the phone, handed it to her.

Her heart thumping, Sarah whispered. "Hello."

Silence.

"Hello," Sarah said again. "Is someone on the line?"

She could hear someone breathing. Then the person on the other end slammed the receiver down.

Her eyes met Ben's. "No one spoke, but it was Mae Peterson, I know it. She is Vivian. She is Mark's fictional Selma. There's no other explanation for her harassment."

Sarah suddenly clapped her hand to her head. "How could I have forgotten!"

"What? What is it?"

"I found a typewritten note in Mark's files. I thought it was part of his manuscript, but the rest of his notes were handwritten and the note used Mark's real name, rather than Matt Layton, his fictional psychiatrist. The note said something to the effect that he had better sleep with one eye open and that the writer hadn't decided who to kill first. Ben, the date on the note was the same date Mark and I were married."

Ben whistled softly. "You're thinking if Mark broke off with Vivian to marry you..."

"She might have wanted to punish us," Sarah said. "Perhaps while he was still single she kept hoping he'd go back to her."

"For three years?"

"I told you, I don't have all the answers."

"Do you want to try to tell the police your suspicions again? Maybe they could figure out probable cause to get a search warrant to search Mae's house."

"No, not yet. It's all speculation. I don't even have Mark's notes or Vivian's letters any longer. I've got to get into Mae's house myself, in case she has Harriet and Emma."

"We can't do anything tonight, because we don't know where she lives. Tomorrow we'll find out, and make a plan."

IN HER NIGHTMARE Sarah was surrounded by flames. Mae Peterson's laughter followed her as she frantically tried to find Emma, who was lost somewhere in the smoke.

Then Harriet appeared and said, "He married beneath him, you know." She didn't seem to realize her hair was on fire.

Sarah tried to fling a blanket over Harriet's head, to snuff out the flames, but then a white-coated doctor moved between them and he was pointing his finger at her.

"No!" Sarah screamed. "This isn't real. I'm dreaming!"

She jumped up onto a chair, reaching for the trapdoor, knowing she must reach daylight so she could wake up. But she slipped, and began falling back into the smoky darkness.

"Sarah, it's all right. I'm here. Sarah, wake up." Ben's voice reached her across the chasm into which she had fallen.

Strong arms held her, and she stopped struggling. Opening her eyes, she saw Ben's face close to hers, his expression anxious. He gently stroked her hair out of her eyes.

For a moment she remained still, trying to bridge the gap between sleep and wakefulness, trying to remember what was real and what she had merely dreamed.

Ben was sitting on the edge of her bed fully dressed. He kept her folded in his arms.

"Nightmare?" he whispered.

She nodded.

"Would you like a glass of water?"

She shook her head. "Just hold me, please."

He held her more closely, his lips pressed to her hair. "You've had more to contend with lately than most people have to deal with in a lifetime."

"Thank you for being here, Ben. I don't think I could have borne this alone."

"You're a lot stronger than you give yourself credit for, but Sarah, you can't stay in this damned house. You're never going to get any sleep here. You've only been in bed an hour. There's not going to be a call from a kidnapper, not after all this time. If Mae's involved, she won't call— not after the visit. Don't you see, if she is Vivian, then she's playing some sort of cat and mouse game with you. There was another hang-up call while you were asleep. I'll hook up the answering machine, then we'll go to my place."

Sarah nodded. "All right. Let me get a few things."

She hastily tossed toilet articles, pajamas, and a change of clothes into an overnight bag. On their way out she stopped at the hall closet to get her hooded parka. All of the clothing was in a heap on the floor of the closet. She sighed and began to rehang jackets and coats.

"My parka isn't here," she said a moment later. "I don't remember moving it. Well, I must have left it upstairs in the bedroom closet."

"Do you want to go and get it?" Ben was waiting by the front door, holding her overnight bag.

"No, I'll get it tomorrow. I can wear this for tonight." She reached for the cashmere coat she had worn to the police station.

BEN INSISTED that she take his bed. He sat beside her, holding her hand. "I'm going to stay with you until you fall asleep. We're going to take your mind off everything but pleasant things, Sarah, because believe it or not, this will all pass."

"I keep expecting to wake up and find it's all a nightmare."

"Don't think about it now. You told me you always wanted to write children's stories. Tell me about the kind of stories you want to write—and by the way, having seen you with Emma, I'd say you make a wonderful mother. You do plan to have children yourself one day, I hope?"

"Oh, yes," Sarah breathed fervently.

She stopped herself in time from adding that Ben was exactly the kind of father she'd like to have for her children. After all, she still had a husband. She deeply believed in the institution of marriage, too. But in view of what she'd learned about Mark lately, the idea of remaining married to him was becoming increasingly distasteful. That thought brought a stab of guilt. She sighed softly.

"You're not going to think sad thoughts, remember," Ben prompted.

"I write my stories in rhyme," Sarah said, forcing herself to answer his earlier question. "I've never tried to have one published, but Emma seemed to like them. I think little children who can't read yet like the sound of rhyming words. I can remember my mother reading Dr. Seuss to me as a child. How I loved his stories and . . ."

Sarah broke off abruptly. She sat up, pushing her hair back over her shoulder. "Meredith and Parker!"

"Who are they? Children's book authors?"

"No, they're private investigators that Mark hired— don't ask me why—to watch me. They wouldn't tell me more than that when I called. A report on their surveillance was supposed to be mailed to Mark. It hasn't arrived yet, but it would take three or four days to get here from the East Coast. Ben, maybe they know a lot more that could help us find Emma and Harriet."

"We'll call them in the morning."

Ben stood up and walked over to the dresser. He returned a moment later, carrying her hairbrush.

Sarah looked at him questioningly.

He grinned. "I'm going to brush your hair to help you relax. I remember that's what my father used to do for my mother when she was tense."

He was right, Sarah thought minutes later, as she began to drift off to sleep, feeling the soft bristles massage her scalp and move gently through her hair, feeling Ben's protective presence beside her.

Her thoughts were only of Ben, his kindness, his strength, and in that floating limbo toward sleep something else about him slipped into her mind. Many of the traits she so admired in Ben had been present in her first, doomed fiancé.

Remembering her lost love was a mistake. She tried desperately to shut out the images of the fire, tried to relax and think only of Ben, but her dead fiancé's face kept superimposing itself over Ben's craggy features—and she drifted.

In the dream she was wearing her wedding dress. Tiny white blossoms cascaded through her dark hair, and a filmy veil floated over her face. She ran up the stairs to where he waited—smiling down at her, his eyes telling her she was beautiful and he loved her.

But why were her feet so heavy? It was such an effort to drag them upstairs, and the staircase was growing longer with every step. When she looked up, the first ominous wisps of smoke obscured his face, wrapping tendrils around his arms as he held them out to her. Then the staircase burst into orange flame! Everything vanished in the white heat of fire!

In the silent screams of sleep she called his name, over and over again. "Sarah, you're okay. You're in my house. No one's going to hurt you here. Remember me? Ben? Please, stop fighting me."

The sound of his voice finally broke through her night terrors. She was still shaking and her face was wet with tears. She realized that she was standing, barefoot, on the wooden floor of Ben's bedroom, and Ben was holding her by her wrists.

As she calmed down, his grip relaxed and he enclosed her in his embrace. He wore only pajama pants, his chest was bare, and as her cheek touched his skin she felt him catch his breath. Still disoriented from the nightmare and glad that the man with her was alive, and whole, she slipped her arms around him.

"We'd better get you back into bed before you catch a chill," Ben said in a strangely husky voice.

He picked her up and carried her to the bed. When he tried to release her, she held on to him. "Don't go. Stay with me."

"Sarah, you don't know what you're saying. If I get into bed with you now...we're both too worked up, I don't know how much restraint we'd be capable of and I don't want to tempt fate. When we make love, and there's nothing on this earth I want more, everything is going to be right. We both know this isn't the time or the place."

She sighed deeply and lay back on the pillow. "You're right, Ben. I was panicked by a recurring dream I have. I wanted to stay awake and yes, I wanted you. But I'm not free, am I? I may never be free to love you."

"Sarah, I...I'd better not say what I want to say, what's in my heart. Not yet. Listen, there's no need for you to go back to sleep yet. Come on, put on a robe and let's go downstairs and I'll make hot chocolate and stoke up the fire and we'll talk or read or play music until you feel sleepy again."

Sarah nodded, and he handed her the woollen robe he had left beside the bed for her use. She took it with trembling fingers, feeling wide awake now and regretting her impulsive words.

They went downstairs and Ben rekindled the fire and placed a log in the grate. Sarah watched the firelight play on his bare chest and shoulders. It turned him into a bronze sculpture as magnificent as those he fashioned with his hands.

It was difficult to imagine Ben had once suffered a disabling accident. That thought brought a strange sense of relief. Perhaps Ben had already had his accident and she had been worrying needlessly that she brought bad luck to the men she cared about.

When the fire was blazing, Ben left her and returned minutes later fully dressed, carrying mugs of hot chocolate. He sat across the room from her, keeping a safe distance between them, and gently led her into talking about her childhood as he related incidents from his. But longing and desire drifted between them like an elusive fragrance.

When at last her eyelids grew heavy and her limbs relaxed, she went upstairs alone and climbed into bed.

This time she fell into a deep, dreamless sleep.

Chapter Sixteen

The rainstorm that had been threatening to strike the coast all the previous day finally hit just before dawn and Sarah awoke to the rattle of rain against the windows. She was in Ben's bed and a clock on the side table informed her, to her astonishment, that it was almost ten o'clock.

Ben's warm woollen robe was on the chair beside the bed and she put it on, tied the sash and rolled up the sleeves to a manageable length.

She found Ben in the kitchen, talking on the phone. "I'll be there in a few days, okay? I can't get away now. Postpone the exhibition if you have to—"

He broke off, catching sight of Sarah. Covering the receiver with his hand, he smiled and said, "Good morning, coffee's still hot. Help yourself."

The way his eyes lit up when he saw her warmed Sarah to her toes. She poured coffee as Ben finished the call and when he hung up she said, "I'm disrupting your whole schedule, aren't I?"

"No," he said firmly. "You are not. I'd rather be with you than answering fool questions in some gallery. To be honest, I don't like the meet-the-artist part of my work. There's always some so-called intellectual who wants to analyze my paintings or sculptures and read all sorts of mythic meaning into them that I never dreamed of.''

Sarah laughed. She felt rested, and despite the weather, the morning seemed to hold the promise of a brighter day.

"How about some ham and eggs?" Ben asked.

"Have you eaten?"

He nodded. "I didn't want to wake you."

"Then I'll just have coffee. I slept so late and I've got to check with the police and the hospital."

Ben indicated a phone on the kitchen wall. "Make the calls while I fix you some hot cereal. You're not going to take on the day without something warm inside you."

Waiting to be connected to ICU, Sarah told Ben, "I remembered that Mae Peterson said she'd rented a house and it was only a couple of blocks from the hospital."

"Shouldn't be too hard to find out which houses were rented recently." Ben stirred oatmeal into hot water as he spoke.

"I've never had a man so intent upon feeding me before," Sarah remarked just before the nurse came on the line. There was no change in Mark's condition. The nurse was a trifle curt, no doubt because so many patients from the bus crash had been brought to ICU.

Hanging up, Sarah said, "I'll call the police from Cliff House, I think. I know I'll sound guilty if I call from here."

Ben didn't argue the point. "I'll go up there with you after you've eaten."

She sat down at the table and sipped coffee, marveling at the restorative powers of a night's sleep. Her mind felt clear and she felt strong enough to deal with whatever the day brought.

"I'll get the number of those private investigators and call them, too."

Ben brought her a bowl of steaming oatmeal, along with brown sugar and a pitcher of cream. He sat down opposite to her and watched her pick up the spoon and taste the cereal.

"Mmm, Ben, this is delicious," she said appreciatively. "I don't remember you listing porridge among your culinary accomplishments."

He shrugged modestly and glanced at the rain slashing against the windows. "I'll get you some rain gear while you eat. I don't want you to get that pretty coat drenched."

SARAH SHIVERED as she followed Ben into the damp chill of Cliff House. "I must turn up the heat."

Ben helped her take off the hooded poncho he had provided and put it on the hall stand. "I hooked up the answering machine to your kitchen phone."

In the kitchen, he said, "The red light's blinking, you've got a message."

He pressed the message retrieval button.

Sarah caught her breath, moving closer as Harriet's voice spoke from the machine. "Sarah, this is…Mrs. Lasiter. I'm warning you that if you ever bother Emma or me again I shall…take out a…a restraining order against you. I am never going to subject the child or myself to your abuse again."

Sarah felt her mouth sag. She had to grip the kitchen table to steady herself. The answering machine beeped and whined. Ben snapped it off.

"Ben, I swear I never did anything…"

"Of course you didn't. Harriet must be in on whatever scheme Vivian cooked up."

"No, no, I don't think so," Sarah said urgently. "Play the message again, please."

She listened for a second time. "Her voice sounds terribly strained and you notice how she hesitates before she says 'Mrs. Lasiter'? Ben, she never called herself Mrs. Lasiter to me. From the first time I met her she insisted I call her Harriet. She pauses again, several times, which is not her usual speech pattern. I know it's not much to go on, but I think somebody forced her to make that call. I should have stayed here. If I'd answered the phone she might have given me some other clues."

"Remember the hang-up calls last night? I think they were waiting for you to be gone to leave the message. They didn't want you to have an opportunity to speak to her."

"But how could they know you'd put in an answering machine for me? Harriet knew I *didn't* have one before she left."

Ben's gaze flickered around the room, to the doorway, then the windows. "Somebody must be watching the house."

"How? From where? We're all alone up here. We would have seen a car surely?"

"Not if somebody was dropped off—there are plenty of places to hide, in the pines, or in a cave in the cliffs, with a pair of binoculars. Cliff House is practically all windows, and most of them aren't curtained or shuttered."

"But wouldn't the police have spotted whoever it was during their search?"

"He—or she—might already have left. Or he could have gone inland when the cops showed up, away from the cliff. There's a fire road he could have taken to get to a point farther down the hill without being seen. The searchers were concentrating on the cliffs and main road because the firebreak is rough, unpaved, and you'd have to be pretty nimble to negotiate it. I doubt an elderly lady and a little girl could, which is probably why the rescue team just made a fast pass with the chopper on that side of the hill. However, a fairly agile adult could have climbed down the firebreak and been picked up at the bottom of the hill by an accomplice in a car."

Sarah shivered. "If your theory is correct, then we're dealing with more than one person. What can I do about this message? If I tell the police, it will sound like Harriet ran away because I was abusing them—and the search will be called off."

"This isn't what you want to hear, Sarah, but my advice is to tell Detective Elliot everything. He knows more about the case than anyone at this point. While he may not believe you he'll have to investigate. There are sophisticated tests they can run—if not in Emerald Cove, then in the nearest metropolitan police department—that may pick up clues as to where that call was made from. They can analyze Harriet's voice to see if she was under duress when she made the call."

Reluctantly, Sarah picked up the phone and dialed the Emerald Cove Police Department. She was relieved to hear that Detective Elliot was out. She declined to leave a message, saying she would call back later.

She looked at Ben. "I'll try Meredith and Parker now."

But after a brief search of the captain's mess Sarah realized the invoice from the investigators bearing their address and phone number was missing. "Whoever took Mark's files must have taken the bill, too. I'll call directory assistance, they're surely listed."

Minutes later the answering machine of the private investigators informed her that they could not come to the phone.

"It's about one-thirty on the East Coast, they're probably out to lunch," she said.

"Let's drive into town," Ben suggested. "We'll see if we can find the Peterson woman's address and then check in with Elliot."

"My first stop should be the bank, so I can deposit the money," Sarah answered. "I'll just get my parka. It's more comfortable than a coat and poncho."

But her parka wasn't in her bedroom closet, either. Puzzled, she ran downstairs and checked the hall closet again.

Ben appeared at her side. "Lost something?"

"My parka. That brick red one I've been wearing instead of a raincoat, because it's warm and waterproof and has a hood. It seems to be missing. I checked upstairs."

"Maybe you left it somewhere?"

She tried to remember. The only times she had removed it she had been at Cliff House or Ben's house or the hospital. "I don't think so. But I'll ask at the hospital."

"When did you last wear it?"

"The last time it rained. When was that?"

"Couple of days ago. So it was probably here, in the closet, when your intruder tossed the place. Maybe Mae Peterson took it."

"Yes. But it seems an odd thing to steal. Besides, there's a chance someone other than Mae was in the house. Well, I'll worry about it later. Let's go."

They drove down the hill through heavy, windblown rain and Sarah couldn't help worrying about whether Emma and Harriet were warm and dry somewhere and being cared for. She had no doubt in her mind that Harriet had been coerced into making that damning call. Harriet might not have been thrilled that her grandson married his office manager, but she was incapable of the kind of deviousness and cruelty involved in a plot to destroy Sarah's good name, nor would she have frightened Emma in such a manner.

Ben drove to the bank and waited while Sarah opened an account in her own name, since Mark could not sign the signature card, presenting the silk scarf-wrapped bundle of bills to a wide-eyed teller. Then Ben took her to the café on Main Street.

"I want you to wait here while I talk to a couple of people. I'll get more information if you aren't with me. The locals tend to be suspicious of strangers. When I know where Mae Peterson lives, I'll come back for you."

Inside, she was pulling down her hood and blinking raindrops from her eyelashes when she caught sight of a rack of local newspapers standing near the door.

The headline struck her louder than a scream.

"Accident Victim Identified as Nevada Resident."

Fumbling in her purse for a quarter, she snatched a newspaper from the stack and began reading as she made her way to a table.

The body recovered from the rocks below the old Cliff Road has been identified as Henry Peterson, fifty-five, an accountant from Las Vegas, Nevada.

Mr. Peterson had apparently come to Emerald Cove to join his wife, Mae Ann Peterson, a Nevada real estate agent, who arrived recently to take up residence here.

Interviewed by the *Courier* today, Mrs. Peterson expressed shock, saying she had not been expecting her husband to join her for several more weeks as he was closing his office in Las Vegas. Mrs. Peterson told our reporter, "He must have wanted to surprise me."

The police confirm that since no car was found at the scene, Mr. Peterson was probably a passenger in the car driven by Dr. Mark Lasiter, which went off the Cliff Road about a week ago. Dr. Lasiter is currently in a coma in the Emerald Cove Hospital.

Police speculate Mr. Peterson must have been ejected from the car and pitched down the cliff before the car came to a stop in a stand of pines.

Sarah was on her second cup of coffee and had practically memorized the piece when Ben returned. She handed him the newspaper.

"Yes, I know. I saw the headline and stopped at the *Courier* office and spoke to the editor. It seems the Petersons were longtime residents of Las Vegas but Henry wanted to retire to the coast and take up fishing. His wife hoped to sell real estate here, as she did in Nevada. Sarah, she was with the same broker in Las Vegas for over ten years."

"Ten years!" Sarah repeated. "But..."

"It sort of shoots down the theory that she was in New York having an affair with your husband three years ago, doesn't it?"

"Then I was wrong, Mae isn't Vivian. So, why is she harassing me?"

"Sarah," Ben said gently, "you've been under a tremendous strain. Are you reading more into her actions than is really there, do you think?"

Sarah expected this distrust from Detective Elliot, but not from Ben. "You saw what she did to the house."

"Well, you were right about one thing. We don't know it was Mae who broke in. Why would she have waited around outside for you to come home if she'd already ransacked the house?"

"Because she hadn't found what she was looking for—the money. And because she's trying to drive me crazy."

Ben nodded. "It sure looks that way. I was just posing questions the cops are likely to ask if you make any accusations against her. But we still don't know what the connection is between Mae Peterson and your husband."

Sarah let out a frustrated sigh. "No, we don't."

"Or how Henry Peterson came to be in Mark's car. Was Mark in the habit of picking up hitchhikers?"

"No, absolutely not. And besides, would a retired accountant be likely to be out hitchhiking?"

"Maybe, if his car broke down. There's some pretty desolate desert country between Vegas and the coast."

"But Mark flew out to the coast. He didn't buy the car until he arrived here. And if Mark picked up Peterson in town, why would he bring him up the Cliff Road? Your house and ours are the only ones up here."

"Sarah, nothing your husband did makes any sense."

"Ben, did you find out where Mae is living?"

"Yes. She rented a house in town. It's on Dolphin Drive, where there's older cottages, mostly rentals that often stand empty in the winter. Fishermen rent them by the week or month in the summer. I also learned something else. Her brother has moved in with her."

"Her brother?" she prompted.

"Came to comfort her about her husband's death, they say."

"Did you find out anything about him?"

"The *Courier* editor said he arrived while their reporter was interviewing Mae Peterson and he practically kicked the reporter out of the house, which in itself isn't too surprising. The reporter said the brother—Mae called him Boyd—was a hulking brute with a face that looked like it had taken a few too many punches."

Sarah felt a cold chill sweep over her. Boyd. *Bryce,* in Mark's novel, was Selma's boyfriend. What had Mark written about him? *That he was a big bruiser, with the battered face of a boxer and biceps like King Kong.*

Chapter Seventeen

Steam filmed the windows of the café, overlaying clinging raindrops, and obliterating Sarah's view of the street.

She said, "I'm going to call on Mae. If I'm wrong about her, then the least I can do is offer my sympathy for her loss."

"I don't think that's such a good idea. What if she really is Vivian?"

"Aren't you the one who told me that Mae Peterson has been selling Las Vegas real estate for ten years, and couldn't have been in New York having an affair with Mark?"

"I don't want you to put yourself in danger, Sarah. Even if she isn't Vivian, she's been acting pretty strangely. Besides, I don't like the sound of her brother."

"You can either go with me, or take me home and I'll get the rental car and drive myself there. But I am going," Sarah said. "Look, Ben, Mae *invited* me to visit her. What better time than after I read of her terrible loss? I'll go and offer my sympathy. I could even apologize for rebuffing her friendly overtures. I'll buy a cake or a pie to take with me. I have to assure myself that she doesn't have Harriet and Emma there."

"Assuming she did spirit them away, she's hardly likely to have them sitting out in plain view."

"No, but if she invites me in there may be something lying around—or she might let something slip. I have to try, Ben. You see, the presence of this Boyd convinces me more than ever that Mae and Boyd have got to be the fictional Selma and Bryce that Mark wrote about. But apart from that, think about this—Mae was on my driveway last night offering me saltwater taffy, taunting me about Emma and Harriet, never mentioning that her husband had been killed. Isn't that odd behavior for a woman who's just learned her husband's body had been lying down a cliff for days?"

Before Ben could respond, the bell on the café door tinkled and Sarah started as a uniformed police officer entered. He glanced at them as he went to the counter.

"You finished?" Ben asked quietly. Sarah nodded.

Silently they stood up, and Ben helped her pull the poncho over her head.

"Just a minute," Sarah said. "I'm going to buy a cake."

She had to wait until the officer bought a cup of coffee to go, then she ordered a coffee cake. Things would be so much simpler, she thought, if she could just make the police believe her. Outside, Ben helped her into the car, then he drove a couple of blocks in silence, until she asked, "Are you taking me to Dolphin Drive?"

"Against my better judgment, yes."

She sighed. "Well, I keep thinking over the significant details in Mark's notes. I told you he wrote of a psychiatrist's affair with a patient. She, in turn, was involved in what sounds like a violent psychosexual relationship with her boyfriend, whom Mark called Bryce. Selma—the patient—had confided to the psychiatrist that she was present when Bryce killed someone. Then later Bryce is released from prison and shows up in the psychiatrist's office with her."

Ben braked and came to a stop. "And these are the people you want to go and confront?"

"Well, we don't know for sure they are. But we're not going to find out if we don't at least go and talk to them."

"I wish we knew where Mae's selling Las Vegas real estate for ten years fits in."

"My intuition tells me I'm on the right track. Now can we drive on?"

Ben unsnapped his seat belt. "We're here. That's where she lives."

Sarah wiped the steam from her window and looked out. They were parked in front of an older clapboard cottage, surrounded by a chain-link fence and a privet hedge. There were two cars parked on the driveway. She recognized the Mercedes as the one Mae drove, and the older Porsche as the one in which she claimed her "married friend" had had an accident on Cliff Road.

"Well, she seems to be at home," Sarah answered, trying to sound calmer than she felt.

They got out of the car, and Sarah held the bakery box containing the coffee cake under her poncho while Ben opened the gate. As they approached the front door, they could hear the throbbing base of a heavy metal group blaring from a radio.

Ben rang the bell. "I don't know if they'll hear us over that racket."

"Try again," Sarah said.

He pressed the button and kept his thumb in place for several seconds. A moment later the door was opened by Mae Peterson. She wore a satin wrap, loosely knotted as if she had just put it on in order to come to the door.

Her mouth dropped open as she saw who her visitor was, and Sarah thought that at least the element of surprise was on her side. She looked in vain for signs of grief, but could not detect reddened eyes or tear stains on Mae's cheeks. Her hair was swept up into a neat French braid and her makeup was flawless.

Mae recovered quickly. "Well, what d'you know. You found me." She looked at Ben. "Who's this?"

"My neighbor, Ben Travis. Ben, this is Mrs. Henry Peterson."

Ben nodded to Mae as Sarah held up the pink bakery box. "We came by to offer our sympathy. We're so sorry to hear about your husband." She had to shout to be heard over the pounding beat of the music.

The music died abruptly and a man's voice called from inside the house. "Shut the damn door, you're letting icy blasts in here." The accent was pure Brooklyn, Sarah decided.

Mae's eyes flickered over Sarah and then moved to Ben. "Why don't you come in for a minute and meet my brother?"

She held the door open wider and Sarah stepped inside. There was no entry hall, but the living room was screened from the front door by a trellis covered with hanging plants. Behind the trellis the room was furnished with Early American furniture, maple tables, chairs and a sofa covered with faded print slipcovers. A man sprawled on the sofa, a can of beer in one hand and a remote control in the other. There was a CD player next to the television set, which displayed a picture but the sound was muted.

"Hey, Boyd, here's the woman I told you about, the doc's wife, Sarah Lasiter. She brought us a cake and her neighbor—what did you say your name was?"

"Travis. Ben Travis."

Boyd didn't get up. He stared at Sarah. Awkwardly, she set the bakery box on the nearest table. Her poncho was dripping water onto the rug, but no one seemed to notice.

Sarah said, "We heard about Mr. Peterson and came to express our sympathy."

Boyd's eyes were small, deep-set, and Sarah thought of raisins in misshapen dough. Like Mae, he was cadaver pale.

A light flashed on in Sarah's mind. *Prison,* she thought. *He's been in prison again.* Mark wrote that he'd been released from prison while Mae was a patient. Could Mae also have been incarcerated? That would explain why Mark didn't hear from them for three years.

"Yeah, very sad," Boyd said. "Big shock. Mae wasn't even expecting old Henry here yet. I guess you've got a vested interest here, Mrs. Lasiter?"

"I'm not sure I understand what you mean."

"Well, it seems Henry was riding in your husband's car. You must be scared sh—silly we'll sue."

"I think we should leave," Ben said.

Sarah remained rooted to the spot. Except for the patter of rain and moan of the wind, the house was silent without the music. She glanced around the room, hoping for some sign that Emma or Harriet had been here, but there was nothing.

She addressed her response to Mae, speaking loudly in the hope that if Emma and Harriet were in the house they would hear her. "No one knows who or what caused the accident that put my husband in the hospital, or how your husband was killed. It's a little premature to make assumptions until we have all the facts. After all, Mae, you were also involved in an accident, the night you came to my door for help."

Ben took her arm firmly. "Good day, Mrs. Peterson."

Sarah found herself being propelled to the door.

Mae followed. "Don't mind Boyd," she said. "He's just watching out for my interests. Thanks for the cake." She paused, her eyes fixed on Sarah. "Did your little girl like the taffy?"

Sarah swallowed a retort. "She hasn't eaten it yet."

In Ben's car he grimaced. "Charming pair. But I didn't see any sign that they're kidnappers, did you? Why did you bring up her accident on the Cliff Road? She looked at Boyd when you did and I didn't like the undercurrent that flowed between them."

"Don't you see, Henry Peterson could have been in the Porsche with her that night. He could have been killed that night. It was just two nights after Mark's accident. I doubt the medical examiner could pinpoint the time of death within a couple of days, not after the body had been exposed to the elements for a week. You saw Mae—did she look like a grief-stricken widow to you? What if she killed him? If she *is* Vivian and she killed Mark's first wife, then she would be capable of killing again."

"Do you want to try to reach Detective Elliot again?"

"No, not yet. I want to call the private investigators first." Maybe she'd find concrete evidence of the sort the detective couldn't ignore.

"There's a pay phone at the gas station on the corner, or would you rather go back to my place, get out of the rain?"

Sarah considered. "We'd better go back to Cliff House, in case anyone has tried to reach me. I'll call from there. Could we stop at the grocery store and buy something for lunch? For once, I'll cook for you."

Ben smiled. "That's the best offer I've had lately."

ALTHOUGH THE RED LIGHT flashed on the answering machine, there had been only hang-up calls. She stir-fried chicken strips and vegetables for lunch, and cooked rice. The food was delicious, but she was too tense to enjoy the meal, although Ben cleaned his plate and pronounced it excellent.

Afterward, she was successful in reaching Parker, of Meredith and Parker, Investigations. This time she was in no mood for evasion. "Mr. Parker, perhaps I'm not making myself clear. My husband is in a coma. I am being stalked, my stepdaughter and her great-grandmother have disappeared. I have to know why my husband paid you to watch me. I also need to know if the name Vivian means anything to you."

There was a pause on the long distance line, then the private investigator answered, "Okay, I can tell you that the surveillance was for your protection. Your husband asked us to watch you to be sure Vivian Novak didn't approach you."

Sarah felt a small surge of elation. At least she now had a name. "He was afraid she might harm me?"

"Our orders were to be sure she didn't get anywhere near you, or his daughter and grandmother. The assignment was terminated when you left the city."

"Can you describe this Vivian Novak to me?"

"I thought you said you knew her?" His tone was wary now.

"She's changed her name, but I'm sure it is the same woman."

"Look, ma'am, we mailed a full report to your husband. I can't tell you any more over the phone."

"He didn't get the report. Could you send a copy right away? If I could get hold of a fax machine you could—"

"No. We don't send confidential reports by fax. I'll mail you another copy."

"By overnight express—" Sarah started to say, but the line had already gone dead.

Sarah replaced the receiver and looked at Ben. "Vivian Novak. They were supposed to keep her away from Emma and Harriet and me. Oh, Ben, Mark was trying to protect us."

Ben leaned forward and grasped her hands. "If your husband gave up his practice to move clear across the country and paid bodyguards to watch his family because of Vivian, then he must have believed she was extremely dangerous. Doesn't sound like a simple case of blackmail. He would have paid her off in New York. Why run? He must have been afraid she would harm you. That death threat you found was real."

Sarah nodded. "He was hoping to disappear, but instead she found him. So he rented Cliff House but was trying to buy a boat so that as soon as we arrived we could do some sailing and hopefully throw her off our trail. Mark must have decided to try to buy some time until we got here by offering to pay her to leave us alone."

"Instead, his car goes off the road," Ben said slowly. "And when you arrive...somebody tampered with your Jeep."

Shivering, Sarah said, "The blackmail money was just icing on the cake, what she was really after was revenge. Dear God, she wants us all dead.... You were right, Ben, she's playing a cat and mouse game with us, tormenting and torturing us before she kills us! Oh, please, God, don't let her have Emma and Harriet!"

"Don't crack up now, Sarah. You've got to stay strong. First of all, she evidently knows about the money, or she wouldn't have searched the house. If she does have Harriet and Emma—and we have no proof of that—then she might enjoy torturing you with more phone calls like that message on the machine from Harriet, at least until you pay her off."

"What can I do? If I go to the police and they question her, who knows what she might do to Harriet and Emma before we can find them. Ben, she's a psychopath."

"And now she has Boyd to help her," Ben said. "You're right. We can forget about calling Detective Elliot now."

"What are we going to do?" Sarah whispered.

"For one thing, we can call the broker in Las Vegas where Mae Peterson hung her licence for the last ten years and find out how long she was married to Henry, what sort of marriage they had—he was obviously at least twenty years older than she is—and if she left Vegas for any extended periods. At least that way we'd be able to determine if Mae and Vivian could be one and the same woman."

"Yes," Sarah said. "Ben, if she tried to kill Mark..."

"Don't dwell on that now."

She began to tremble uncontrollably.

Ben closed the distance between them and took her in his arms. She looked up at him, and their eyes locked. Neither spoke, but their feelings needed no words.

At length Ben sighed.

Sarah bit her lip and turned away. "I have a husband, Ben."

"Yes," he said heavily. "I know."

Chapter Eighteen

The rain diminished to a gray drizzle by midafternoon. Detective Elliot called to ask if Sarah had heard from Harriet. She begged the detective to keep searching.

Sarah maintained a careful distance from Ben and avoided meeting his gaze, yet she was acutely aware of his presence. She felt his eyes follow her and knew the silent battle he was waging with himself, because she was fighting one of her own. She yearned for the comfort of his touch, but she didn't dare encourage physical contact, because the consequences would be irrevocable.

A call to the real estate brokers in Las Vegas where Mae had been employed generated a curt response. The instant Sarah mentioned Mae Peterson, the receptionist who answered the phone snapped, "I'm not allowed to give out personal information about our Realtors. Please don't call again."

She relayed this to Ben, and, unable to bear the tension, added, "I should go to the hospital and be with Mark."

Ben was silent for a moment. "Maybe that would be a good idea. I'll stay here. I'll wait awhile and then see if I can get any information out of Vegas. I'm not above a little subterfuge—like impersonating an officer."

"Oh, Ben, I'm corrupting you," she said, only half-jokingly. "I still don't know which guardian angel sent you to me, or whether I deserve your help."

She looked at him then and what she saw in his gaze brought a surge of both joy and sadness. *Oh, Ben,* she thought, *I've been looking for you all my life. Why did I have to find you too late?*

Ben said softly, "Sarah there's something mysterious about the way we connect with other people. The spark is there, or it isn't. And after that initial attraction, then we get down to specifics. Like admiring somebody who doesn't run when the going gets rough, who thinks about other people before herself, who doesn't compromise her integrity no matter what, who keeps promises and gives other people the benefit of the doubt...."

He paused and Sarah knew he was referring to her loyalty to Mark. Had it occurred to Ben, as it had to her, that Mark's original intention when he left her in New York might have been to disappear on his own, leaving her to care for his family? Whatever had caused her husband to change his mind and ask her to join him didn't alter the fact that he had departed alone.

Ben went on, "Besides all of that, how can anyone not be impressed by a woman who somehow—I don't know how—manages to stay upbeat and hopeful through events that would do most women in. You know that old question, who would you prefer to be marooned on a desert island with...?"

Sarah smiled in spite of the tension she felt. "Staying upbeat is easier when you know someone's on your side, Ben."

"Count on that, Sarah."

Suppressing a sigh, she said, "I'll see you later."

Driving down the hill, Sarah felt very alone. She missed Ben's reassuring presence. She dared not think about Harriet and Emma, for fear her imagination would run riot, so she forced herself to think about her comatose husband.

She prayed again that Mark would recover soon. That he would wake up and make all her doubts and fears disappear. Or would he confess that he was responsible for this nightmare? Was she judging him too harshly? Could he be innocent of any wrongdoing, the victim of a deeply disturbed woman bent on destroying him?

But Sarah couldn't merely explain away the vividly portrayed affair, described in his handwriting, between psychiatrist and patient. Nor could she account for Vivian's graphically explicit letters.

Mark was a man who enjoyed sex. Her brief marriage had demonstrated that fact. Sarah was not naive enough to believe he had been celibate all the years he was single, and he had succeeded in swiftly, effortlessly, seducing her. He was, she realized now, an expert in the art of seduction.

A memory returned, of an evening shortly before they were married. Mark had come to pick her up to take her to a concert, but they never left her apartment.

It had been a warm summer night and she had a new dress, a white jersey with thin shoulder straps. Mark had stood on the threshold, his eyes traveling slowly over her body. The next moment she was in his arms, the bouquet of roses he had brought were on the floor, and he was sliding her shoulder straps down her arms.

They had made love. And much later, as she lay in his arms he had told her how much he adored her for her spontaneity, and had made a remark that came back to haunt her now. He had murmured that it was wonderful to find a woman who shared his passion, because his first wife had been less responsive. It was one of the rare occasions he had spoken of Tamara.

Now Sarah wondered if he had thought that gave him an excuse to have an affair.

At the hospital she was informed that Mark had been moved from ICU to a private room, as his condition, although comatose, was stable enough that he did not require the ICU facilities, which were needed for the influx of accident victims.

Sarah was glad of the privacy. She checked the locker and saw that the leather jacket Mark had been wearing at the time of his accident had been placed on a hanger. The jacket was torn and stained. A cardboard box contained the tattered remains of his jeans and shirt, which appeared to have been cut from his body. The dark patches were unmistakably bloodstains. There was only one shoe and his socks were missing. She hastily closed the door.

Pulling a chair close to the bed, she sat down.

The monitor behind Mark registered all of the blips and beeps of his life support system and an IV dripped into his arm. Staring at the stranger in the bed, Sarah felt pity, and a deep compassion, but no real connection. She and Mark had been together for such a brief time as husband and wife. It was easier to recall him as her doctor, then as her employer, than as her husband.

There were different levels of betrayal, she thought, as all of the nuances of Mark's various betrayals began to coalesce with chilling clarity.

He had probably betrayed his first wife by having an affair with a patient, and at the same time he had betrayed his profession, violating his Hypocratic oath. He had also betrayed Vivian, who had gone to him for counseling and instead been seduced by his false promises.

Lastly, Sarah thought, he had betrayed her by drawing her into the web being spun around him by a madwoman.

But after a few minutes her own guilt returned. She had to take the blame for Emma's disappearance. Mark had placed the child in her care and she had not been able to protect her.

If only she knew for certain that Emma had not been taken away by Harriet. If only Mark could tell her if Harriet was capable of turning on her like that.

Wake up, Mark, she thought. *Wake up and tell me what to do.*

But the bandaged-swathed figure on the bed remained still and silent.

WHEN SARAH RETURNED to Cliff House Ben met her at the door and helped her take off her coat. "Good to have you back."

"I don't think I could have faced the house if you hadn't been here," Sarah answered.

She slipped her cashmere coat onto a hanger. It had been a gift from Mark and had never been intended to be worn in wind-driven rain. The collar was damp and she saw she had a mud splatter on the hem. She wondered again what had become of her rugged parka, which was far more suitable for the howling gales that struck this part of the northern California coast in winter.

Ben had lit a roaring fire in the living room fireplace and had miraculously produced steaks and a portable indoor barbecue. He had potatoes baking in the oven and had chopped cabbage for coleslaw. She smiled appreciatively. "You've been busy."

"Gave me something to do. How's your husband?"

"The same."

They regarded each other awkwardly for a moment, keeping at arm's length, then Sarah walked into the living room, rubbing her hands and extending them toward the fire.

Ben had found a box and covered it with a sheet. On the makeshift table he had set out plates and cutlery and napkins. "I intended to bring a bottle of wine up from my place when I went for the food, but I forgot, and didn't want to be gone when you came back. I'll go get it now."

"No, don't leave," Sarah said quickly. "I believe there's a bottle of wine in one of the kitchen cabinets that survived the ransacking," Sarah answered. "But . . ."

"But you don't think you should enjoy any small pleasures under the current circumstances," Ben finished for her.

"Something like that, I suppose."

"Okay, let's forget the wine. Let me tell you about an interesting call to the Vegas real estate office. I finally got hold of a live person. She was a fairly new agent but she knew the Petersons. It seems that although Henry Peterson was planning to retire and move to Santa Barbara, he intended to wait until after tax season in late April. Mae was going to scout a place for them to live and was expected back in a couple of weeks."

"Santa Barbara," Sarah repeated. "So they never intended to come to Emerald Cove."

"No, their destination was central California. She was going to find a house to buy and open an escrow, then go back to Vegas while the escrow proceeded. The agency was surprised when they received a postcard from Emerald Cove saying Mae intended to stay here indefinitely."

Ben paused. "The next thing they knew, Henry abruptly closed down his office to join her. I also asked the agent I spoke to if she knew Mae's brother, Boyd. She said she didn't, but that she hadn't been with the office very long."

Sarah followed Ben into the kitchen. While he placed the steaks on the grill, she found a bottle of wine and began searching for a corkscrew, telling herself that having a glass of wine was hardly a celebration. Besides, it would help banish the damp chill of the house. "Did you ask if she knew whether or not Mae had spent any extended periods away from Las Vegas?"

Ben frowned. "Yes. She said someone had told her that the Petersons came out to the coast for two weeks every summer without fail. That they were a devoted couple, inseparable, and this was the first time Mae had ever traveled on her own."

Sarah stared at him. "That doesn't sound much like the Mae Peterson I've been dealing with. Ben, is it possible—"

"I've been wondering the same thing," Ben replied over the sizzle of the steaks. "It didn't occur to me at the time to ask what their Mae Peterson looked like and by the time I did think of it, the real estate office was closed for the day. We'll do it first thing in the morning."

Sarah looked away quickly. She didn't want to spend the night alone in Cliff House, yet could not ask Ben to stay with her, nor invite herself to spend a second night at his house. Their growing attraction for each other was creating a sexual tension that was impossible to ignore.

Ben was watching her and she was startled when he said, "No, I'm not going to leave you here alone, Sarah. No one's going to know if I bunk down here and you sleep upstairs. Or we could go back to my place, if you like."

"We'll talk about that after we eat, Ben. I do have to get used to being alone, at least until Mark recovers."

Was she invoking her husband's name as a means of defense against her growing attraction to Ben? she wondered. She found two wineglasses and carried them into the living room. Ben followed and began to open the bottle of wine.

Sarah was about to sit on the floor in front of the fire, then remembered there was no telephone extension in the unfurnished room. She went to the captain's mess, unplugged the phone, and took it back with her, placing it on the floor beside Ben's improvised dining table.

While they ate, they both made a conscious effort to keep the conversation light, and impersonal, but Sarah glanced frequently in the direction of the telephone. She tried to force down the meat, but could manage only a couple of bites, then spent several minutes mashing her potato.

At last she jumped to her feet and began to pace around the room. "I can't stand the waiting, Ben! I keep seeing Emma everywhere I look—I keep hearing her voice. Oh, dear God, I must know she's all right. She's only four years old! She's a baby. I'm more worried about the child than the father and—"

Ben was on his feet, closing the distance between them. He caught her and pulled her close to him. "Sarah, it's okay, cry, scream, whatever you need to do to get it out."

A sob was trapped in her throat. She said raggedly, "We mustn't . . . be together . . . like this."

"I've wanted to hold you ever since you came back from the hospital. Sarah, I've ached to hold you. Don't push me away. Let me comfort you."

"No, Ben, please, don't," Sarah whispered. "It isn't you that I don't trust, it's myself."

His eyes sought and found hers, held her gaze. His hands went to her face, cradling her cheeks so that she could not look away. "Forgive me, Sarah, but I have to say it. You married a man who betrayed your trust. He didn't tell you about his past, or that he and everyone close to him were in danger. I pity him for being injured. I hope he recovers, but Sarah, he doesn't deserve you."

She wrenched herself from his arms. "Please go, Ben. Whatever he might have done, he is my husband. I've got to be loyal to him and to my marriage vows. When he's well again..."

"Just let me say this, Sarah, however long it takes...I'll be here."

Sarah turned her head away, so he wouldn't see the tears stinging her eyes.

She felt Ben's hand lightly touch her arm. "Come on, try to eat something. You've got to keep up your strength."

They returned to the food and Sarah made an effort to eat. Afterward they carried the dishes into the kitchen. Once the dishes were done and put away, Sarah began to nervously clean the surfaces of counters and straighten drawers. Sensing her need to keep busy, Ben made no comment.

When she was at last satisfied that the kitchen was spotless she announced. "I'm going to bake cookies. Emma loves cookies."

"I'll go and put another log on the fire."

An hour later trays of oatmeal and chocolate chip cookies were cooling and Sarah, her burst of nervous energy expended, was sitting on the floor in front of the living room fire.

Ben brought her a glass of wine. "Maybe this will help you relax."

She nodded. "Thank you."

"Sarah, I've got to ask you—the nightmares you've been having. You said they were recurring dreams. I presume they're not new—I mean, not about what's happened here.''

She shook her head. ''I dream about the fire that killed my parents and my fiancé.''

All at once it seemed the floodgates of memory opened and she began to tell him of her anguish and grief, of the guilt that still haunted her. She was able to tell Ben things she had never even told Mark when he was counseling her, including how much she had loved the man she had been fated never to marry.

Lastly, she looked at Ben through eyes misted with tears and said, ''You remind me so much of him, Ben, although you don't look alike. All of your quiet strength, your creativity, your kindness . . . the way we are able to talk, to be at ease with each other, even under the most trying circumstances. I hadn't realized how much I missed that. With Mark I was awed, overwhelmed, flattered, infatuated . . . but looking back, I realize I was never truly comfortable or at ease with him.''

Ben smiled. ''I feel the same way. If we can get along this well under the present circumstances, imagine how great it would be in more tranquil times. Do you realize, by the way, that it's after ten? Are you getting tired?''

''A little. But I don't want to leave the fire, or you, just yet.''

The telephone rang, causing Sarah to jump. She grabbed the receiver. ''Sarah Lasiter.''

''Mrs. Lasiter? This is Emerald Cove Hospital.''

She felt her entire body tense. Drawing a deep breath, she said, ''Yes, this is Mrs. Lasiter. Is my husband . . . awake?''

There was a pause. ''Could you come down here? The doctor would like to speak with you.''

''What is it? What happened?''

"I'm sorry, Mrs. Lasiter, but you'll have to speak with the doctor when you get here."

"I'm on my way," Sarah said.

BEN DROVE HER to the hospital and he went to the waiting room while Sarah hurried to Mark's room. Catching sight of her, one of the nurses left her station and barred the way.

"Dr. Conroy would like to see you in his office, Mrs. Lasiter."

Suddenly panicked, Sarah said, "I want to see my husband first."

The nurse said firmly, "This way, Mrs. Lasiter."

Sarah could see that the door to Mark's room was closed. She allowed the nurse to usher her into an office and close the door.

Dr. Conroy was seated behind his desk, but rose immediately and came to her. Sarah knew instantly that he was about to deliver the worst possible news.

"My husband's dead, isn't he?"

The doctor nodded gravely. "I'm sorry."

"When? When did it happen? Did you know it was going to happen? Why didn't you call me?"

"There was no warning, Mrs. Lasiter." He paused. "He flatlined—that is, the monitors showed his heart stopped beating shortly after you visited him this evening."

Was she imagining a veiled accusation in his tone?

"This evening? I was here this *afternoon,* not this evening."

He wore gold-rimmed glasses, behind which his gray eyes were mirrors that seemed to reflect back to her all of her shock and pain. "Mrs. Lasiter, sometimes the stress of dealing with severe illness and injury causes us to lose track of time. But the night nurse was just starting her rounds and she did remark to me that it was a shame that you had left only minutes before she went to check on your husband.''

Sarah's knees suddenly felt weak and she collapsed into the nearest chair. ''She was mistaken. I was not here this evening.''

''Well, it doesn't make any different now, does it? Mrs. Lasiter . . . this is painful to you, I know, but there are certain formalities to be observed.'' He returned to his seat and opened a file on his desk.

''Yes, of course,'' she whispered. ''I'll sign whatever you need. May I go to my husband now?''

He hesitated. ''Not yet. The medical examiner must examine him first.''

''An autopsy?'' The implication dawned on her then.

''It's usual in the case of sudden death. We need to know the exact cause of death and then I can sign the certificate and so on.''

''But surely I can be with him for just a minute—''

''It's late, Mrs. Lasiter. Why don't you go home. I can give you a sedative, if you like. We'll be in touch in the morning and you can make all the necessary arrangements then.''

Sarah stood up and walked out, feeling like a zombie.

Chapter Nineteen

Ben took her back to his house, gave her hot chocolate, then tucked her into bed. She was too numb to argue, and grateful to have someone take charge. Besides, the idea of spending the night alone at Cliff House was abhorrent to her.

Still, despite Ben's best efforts, she awoke with a start almost every hour during the night. When an overcast dawn broke, she slipped on Ben's robe and tiptoed down to the kitchen. She was surprised to find he was already up. Wordlessly, she walked to him and laid her head against his chest.

He folded her into his arms. "Did you get any sleep?"

"A little."

"The doctor should have given you a sedative."

"He offered one...Ben, part of me can't believe Mark's gone and grieves for him and at the same time another part of me is angry that he's taken all his secrets to the grave with him."

"That's understandable, Sarah. You've got to stop being so hard on yourself. Come on, sit down and I'll pour you a cup of coffee. I guess you want to get down to the hospital as soon as possible."

"Thank you." She was about to add that she'd take a quick shower and get dressed first when his doorbell rang.

"I'll get it. Why don't you pop some bread in the toaster? We can eat it on the way."

Sarah had just taken two slices from a loaf of bread when she heard Ben say, "Yes, she's here. How about waiting outside while I get her."

A muffled response was made in a vaguely familiar voice, then Ben reappeared at the kitchen door.

"It's Detective Elliot. He insists on seeing you right away. I tried to stall him but he says it's urgent. He's waiting in the hall so there's no way you can get upstairs to your clothes."

Sarah glanced down at the obviously male robe she was wearing, color flooding her cheeks. "I can't see him like this."

But it was too late. The detective had followed Ben and was now standing on the threshold.

"Forgive the intrusion," Elliot said in a voice that expressed anything but apology, "but I must speak with you in private immediately, Mrs. Lasiter."

"Whatever you have to say, you can say in front of Mr. Travis."

"No, as a matter of fact, I can't. Will you get dressed quickly, please, and accompany me to Cliff House?"

"Why? I mean, why can't you tell me whatever it is you want to say here and now?"

"Mrs. Lasiter, I have a warrant to search Cliff House. I'd like you to open it up for me."

"A search warrant? But what are you going to look for?"

"You can either get dressed or come as you are." His tone brooked no argument.

"Sarah," Ben said. "Why don't you go along with him? I'll wait here. Call me if you need anything."

Scarcely aware of what she was doing, Sarah ran up to Ben's room and flung on her clothes. Waiting at the foot of the stairs, the detective's eyes went over her mud-spattered cashmere coat, but he made no comment.

Outside she started toward her car, which was still parked on Ben's driveway, but Elliot insisted that she ride with him. Two uniformed officers were waiting at Cliff House and Sarah unlocked the front door and let them in.

She turned to face the detective. "Now will you please tell me what you're looking for? Perhaps you aren't aware, but my husband died last night. I need to go to the hospital."

Elliot's catlike gaze flickered over her face, as if measuring her sincerity. "You husband died last night and you spent the night with Ben Travis?"

She felt a surge of guilt and stammered, "I—I spent the night at his house. I was upset . . . it isn't what you're implying."

"I suppose Travis is going to vouch for your whereabouts all evening?"

"Vouch? Why should he have to. . ."

"Your husband was murdered last night."

Before the impact of what Elliot said could register, he continued, "A saline IV drip was switched for a lethal solution of morphine and heroin. This killed him without the monitors hooked to the life support system alerting the hospital staff as they would have had the machines simply been unplugged. Since heroin isn't used in hospitals, someone took the drug in from the outside."

For an instant the room swam out of focus.

The detective was speaking again, but his words didn't register. Only one word hammered on her brain. *Murdered. Murdered.*

She tried to concentrate on what Elliot was saying.

"Pretty tough, dealing with the situation you found yourself in," Elliot continued in a deceptively soft tone. "Enough to push anybody over the edge."

"Situation? Do you mean my husband's coma, or the disappearance of his daughter and grandmother?"

Elliot's expression was blank, neither judgmental nor sympathetic. "Mrs. Harriet Lasiter called us inquiring about restraining orders."

"What?"

"She said she was afraid you might go after her and force her and the child to return to you. She said she couldn't allow that to happen. That it was difficult enough to live with you while your husband was around but without his protection she feared for her safety and that of the child."

Sarah's heart began to thud wildly against her ribs. "I have never abused nor threatened either of them, in any way, ever. How do you know it was my husband's grandmother who called? Detective, I told you about the woman named Mae Peterson. I'm certain she has something to do with this...this plot, conspiracy, whatever it is. Please, will you at least interview her?"

Ignoring her, Elliot pulled a small notebook from his pocket and studied several entries. "Your husband was considerably older than you, wasn't he?"

"Fifteen years. What are you implying?"

"The prognosis for his recovery wasn't hopeful, I take it? He could have stayed in a coma for years."

"I never gave up hope," she said. "People come out of deep comas all the time."

"Tough for a young attractive woman to be tied to a man who might be a vegetable for years." He paused, gave her another piercing glance and added, "Especially if she's met someone else."

"How dare you—"

He was relentless, not giving her an opportunity to respond, "Mrs. Lasiter, you were seen leaving your husband's room last evening shortly before he flat-lined."

"I was not at the hospital last evening. I was there in the afternoon."

"Where were you between four-thirty and eight last night?"

She couldn't meet his eye. He'd found her at Ben's house, clad in Ben's robe. "I came straight home—well, to Mr. Travis's house—from the hospital."

"You worked for your husband before you married him, right?"

"Yes. Who told you that?"

"Harriet Lasiter. Now, let me see, working for a psychiatrist you would have knowledge of drugs—he probably treated addicts and, of course, a psychiatrist is a medical doctor who could prescribe drugs, probably kept drugs in the office."

The detective seemed to emphasize the word *drugs,* and as he repeated it, Sarah wanted to cover her ears. The implication clearly was that after working in a doctor's office she would have had sufficient knowledge of drugs to concoct a lethal cocktail of morphine and heroin.

"I was his office manager, not his nurse. And in any event, heroin isn't prescribed by psychiatrists."

"Now, you and Ben Travis—"

"We're not having an affair."

He raised an eyebrow. "Did you surmise I was about to say you were?" His tone was sarcastic. "What could possibly have given me that idea?"

Sarah could hear the two uniformed officers going from room to room, opening and closing doors and drawers, dragging furniture about. It didn't sound as if they were being particularly careful. "What are your men searching for? Evidence of a crime?"

"You spent the night with Ben Travis, isn't that what you told me?"

Motive, Sarah thought, panicked. *He's certain I killed Mark. He thinks I married him for money and position, that I didn't love him enough to stand by him... that I now want Ben.*

One of the officers came down the stairs and walked over to the guest closet in the hall. He started to go through it, pulling out coats, examining pockets, piling everything on the floor. He was no more careful than her intruder had been.

Sarah watched angrily, feeling violated.

At length the officer turned to Elliot. "No sign of the brick-colored parka the night nurse said she was wearing."

"I lost that parka," Sarah said quickly. "I must have left it somewhere, or—" She broke off. If she told him now that someone had broken into Cliff House, ransacked it, and made off with her parka, it would sound like a ridiculous excuse.

Swallowing hard, she said, "Ben Travis will tell you that I was with him yesterday from about five o'clock on. Between four-thirty and five I was on my way from the hospital."

"I'll have a word with Travis later." Elliot looked at the two officers, who were waiting expectantly. One of them was now holding a brown paper bag. "You finished? Okay, go ahead."

When he faced Sarah again he studied her silently for an interminable minute, perhaps expecting her to make some incriminating statement.

Unable to stand the tension, she burst out, "Aren't you supposed to read me my rights?"

"You're not under arrest, Mrs. Lasiter." The unspoken word *yet* hung in the air. "I'll probably have some more questions for you later on. Will you be here or at Travis's house?"

"I don't know where I'll be," Sarah answered coldly.

BEN ARRIVED fifteen minutes after the police left. "What were they looking for?"

"My missing parka, among other things. Ben, somebody switched Mark's IV for a lethal solution of morphine and heroin. He was murdered and they think I did it." She related all she could remember of the exchange between Elliot and herself.

Ben listened with growing consternation. "They probably want to check the parka for traces of the drugs. You don't know what they took away in the brown paper bag?"

Sarah shook her head. "I haven't checked."

"Would your husband have brought any drugs with him—prescription drugs, for instance?"

"I didn't unpack any. Harriet took a prescription drug for her high blood pressure, that's all."

"Maybe that's what the cops took."

Sarah pressed her palm to her forehead. "I don't know what to do. I can't believe Harriet called the police and asked about restraining orders. Is it possible? Did I misjudge her that much?"

"How can they be certain it was Harriet who called? And even if it was, if Mae Peterson has her she could have forced her to make the call with threats to harm Emma."

Sarah glanced at the open closet door, and the clothes that were dumped on the floor. Shivering, she wrapped her arms around herself. "I hate this house. I wish I'd never come here."

Ben pulled her, unresisting, into his arms. "Vivian Novak—alias Mae Peterson, might have found you no matter where you went. Besides, if you hadn't come here I'd never have met you and I don't even want to think about that. Sarah, when you walked into my life, the future suddenly became appealing, exciting, somewhere I wanted to go."

"I didn't kill my husband, Ben. I swear I didn't."

"I know you didn't. Come on, let's get out of here. This place gives me the creeps, too. There's no longer any point in trying to hide the fact that we're friends, Sarah."

"Elliot believes we're more than friends, Ben."

She looked up at him. His face was inches from hers. For once she didn't turn away.

Ben gave a long sigh, clearly battling with his conscience, then his lips found hers. His mouth was warm, the kiss as sweet as she'd known it would be, and she melted against him. For one blissful moment she felt fear and tension slip away. Out of all the terror and uncertainty, she had found Ben. His kiss, his touch, promised that somehow they would come through it all.

Reluctantly Ben released her mouth. For an instant they stared at each other in startled wonder, then he said hoarsely, "I'm sorry. I shouldn't have done that."

"And I shouldn't have cooperated, but I did. I shouldn't have done a lot of things, especially let you get involved with me and my problems. Yet . . . if I could go back, I'm not sure I would have acted any differently and that knowledge is filling me with guilt."

"You've done nothing to be ashamed of, Sarah. Don't castigate yourself for a spontaneous kiss. We needed to remind ourselves that there's hope for the future." He paused. "Our future. But I know this isn't the time to talk about it, and perhaps that's why I kissed you just now. Because it's too soon to put into words what I feel for you."

"Ben," Sarah said softly, "you'll never know how much I needed you to give me that unspoken message."

"Much as I'd like to repeat it," Ben said with a wry smile, "right now we have to face the fact that the cops are probably trying to build a case against you. In murder cases close family members are always the prime suspects, and the first twenty-four hours in an investigation are critical. When they have what they believe to be sufficient evidence, they'll issue a warrant. We have to act quickly.

"If Mae doesn't have Harriet, we've got to find her and make her tell you the truth about Mark's past. Then we have to prove that Mae Peterson was stalking him and then turned on you. It was probably Mae, wearing your parka, and maybe a dark wig, who slipped into Mark's room and switched the saline drip. Once he was put into a private room the nurses didn't have to check visitors in and out as they did in ICU. They'd have only noticed the parka and maybe the hair color."

A tear of relief slipped down Sarah's cheek. "In spite of everything, you still believe in me. Oh, Ben, thank you."

Chapter Twenty

"I haven't checked the mail," Sarah said as they left Cliff House. "I'll go and look in the box and then follow you down the hill."

"Okay, I'll get breakfast started."

Walking to the end of the driveway to the mailbox, Sarah was only vaguely aware of the vast, brooding presence of the ocean. The gray dawn held the threat of more rain; the sky was swollen with dark clouds and the air saturated with moisture.

She pulled her coat closer to her body and walked more quickly. Flipping open the mailbox she grabbed a large manila envelope and saw with relief that it was from Meredith and Parker, the private investigators Mark had hired.

Gathering up the rest of the mail, which appeared to be more bills, she ran to her car. She briefly considered reading the report before driving down to Ben's house, but the car was icy cold and from the heft of the manila envelope, the report was lengthy. She'd wait until she was in Ben's warm kitchen to read it. Ben had left his front door slightly ajar for her and when she knocked and stepped inside she could hear him speaking on the phone.

"…yes, I'll go to the police with this right away. I'm sure they'll be in touch with you. Thanks for the information."

He put down the phone as Sarah entered the kitchen and gave her a triumphant smile. "Mae Peterson, licensed real estate agent of Las Vegas, Nevada," he paused, "is a fifty-two-year-old woman, height about five-two, plump, gray-haired."

Sarah sat down abruptly. "Then . . ."

"The tall blonde who says she is Mae Peterson is an imposter."

"And is probably Vivian Novak. What does this mean—how and why would she be masquerading as a fifty-two-year-old woman?"

"Stop and think, Sarah. She shows up here driving an expensive car with Nevada plates, which is undoubtedly registered to Mae Peterson. Our tall blonde doesn't seem to be short of money and I'd lay odds if we were to call a few places in town we'd find out that she's been using credit cards issued in the name of Mae Peterson."

"But how . . ."

"I just spoke to Mae's broker. She described Mae as the most outgoing, friendly woman on earth, a do-anything-for-anybody sort of person. I asked if she was in the habit of picking up hitchhikers and her broker said she did it all the time."

Sarah caught her breath. "You think she picked up Vivian, who then stole her car and credit cards, and took her identity?"

"I think she did more than that," Ben said grimly. "A car and credit cards would have been reported stolen right away. That is, if the owner was *able* to report the thefts."

"Dear God! Do you think she killed the real Mae Peterson?"

"I don't know if you've ever been to Las Vegas, but Mae had to drive across miles of open desert. There are plenty of places where Vivian could have killed her and buried the body in a shallow grave in the sand. The broker said Mae's husband, Henry, didn't at first get upset that his wife hadn't called him because he received a postcard from her saying she had a bad case of laryngitis and would call when she got her voice back.''

"He would have recognized his wife's handwriting," Sarah said. "Which means that Vivian forced Mae to write that postcard.... Oh, how diabolical! She must be forcing Harriet to make these calls, and when she tires of the game...or when she gets her hands on the money she knows Mark was going to give her..."

Sarah didn't dare finish the prediction.

Ben said, "Henry finally got worried that she hadn't called and tracked her down here. But she was moving from place to place at first, from a motel to the B-and-B to the hotel. Eventually she rented the house on Dolphin and Henry got the phone number. When he called, a strange female answered the phone and said Mae was still suffering from laryngitis and that she was taking care of her. Thoroughly alarmed by this time, Peterson promptly dropped everything and drove out here. That was the last the broker, or apparently anyone else in Vegas, heard from him.''

"Because he'd had an accident on the Cliff Road, just like Mark, and just like Mark he had encountered Vivian Novak and her friend Boyd."

"One last detail I forgot to mention. I asked what kind of car Henry Peterson drove. It seems the Petersons liked German cars. He was driving an old Porsche."

Sarah felt an icy chill ripple up her spine. "She killed him the night she came to me at Cliff House and asked for a doctor. The night I drove her to town...Boyd must have been here then...probably watching us as we stopped to check the Porsche, then after we left he drove it away."

Ben said, "No matter what Elliot thinks, we've got to try going to the police again."

Sarah placed the bulky manila envelope from the private investigators on the table in front of her. "First, we'd better read this."

Ben brought coffee to the table and pulled a chair next to her as she opened the envelope.

The report was topped by a short letter addressed to Sarah, but for a moment she ignored both the letter and the computer-printed report. Her heart began to race as she picked up a smaller envelope addressed to her in Mark's handwriting. Attached to the envelope was a yellow Post-it note, on which Meredith had scrawled: "This just reached our office."

Suddenly afraid to see what Mark had written, she glanced at the investigators' letter. It stated that they had only just received the enclosed letter Dr. Lasiter had mailed from California, and in view of the circumstances Sarah had described to them on the phone, and because of the inscription on the envelope, they were including it with their report.

Lifting the Post-it note Sarah read what Mark had written above her name: "Open only in the event of my death."

Sarah felt Ben's hand reassuringly on her shoulder as with shaking fingers she tore open the letter and began to read.

Dear Sarah,

If you are reading this, I am probably dead. Forgive me for dragging you into this nightmare.

You must at all costs take Emma and Harriet to a safe place. Change your names and begin a new life. Under no circumstances allow a woman named Vivian Novak anywhere near any of you.

You see, Vivian Novak was a patient of mine during the time I was married to Tamara. I am ashamed to admit we had an affair. There's nothing I can say to explain or excuse my behavior, other than to say that after years of studying and treating aberrant behavior, perhaps I became—for a little while—inured to it. When I came to my senses and tried to break off the affair, Vivian threatened to tell Tamara everything.

I had no choice, I had to confess to my wife. The result was that Tamara left me, taking Emma, who was a baby at the time, with her.

Although I told Vivian I would not see her again, she refused to believe the affair was over. She decided that it was not Tamara, but Emma, I wanted back, and swore she would get my daughter back for me and we would form a new family.

God forgive me, I should have warned Tamara that Vivian was dangerously unstable, deeply disturbed. But I didn't.

Vivian showed up on my doorstep one day with Emma in her arms. I was horrified that she had kidnapped the baby, but there was worse to come. The police called to tell me my wife was dead, an apparent suicide.

I was beside myself—I knew my wife would never have willingly given up Emma. I didn't believe either that Tamara had killed herself, despite her depression over my infidelity and our breakup. The only other explanation was that Vivian had killed her and taken the baby. I pretended to the police that Tamara had asked me to take the baby for a few days and I had been too stupid to realize what she planned to do.

I know you will be asking now why I didn't tell the police everything. I was a coward, I feared the disgrace if the whole sordid story came out; the censure of my colleagues, the loss of my profession. I love my work, I didn't want to give it up because of my indiscretion with a patient. Besides, I had no proof Vivian had killed Tamara.

But neither could I allow Vivian to continue to harass me and threaten my family. So I had her committed to a psychiatric hospital as a danger to herself and others. I said she had assaulted me and forced her way into my office and my home, which was true. Her behavior when she was first admitted to the psychiatric facility certainly bore this out, as she attacked several staff members and had to be restrained.

I honestly believed this commitment was best for Vivian, too, as I was sure she would get the appropriate treatment. She would also be removed from the destructive relationship with her drug-addicted boyfriend.

Vivian spent three years in the hospital. During the last year she seemed to make remarkable progress, and was clever enough to convince her doctors of her sanity. The last few months she was even working as a nurse's aid.

My rude awakening came shortly after you became my office manager and we started seeing each other, Sarah. I began to receive various objects in the mail— I won't go into detail—but my suspicions as to their origin were confirmed when I learned Vivian had been released. About that time I began to get whispered death threats, late at night at home, which continued even after I changed the phone number to an unlisted one.

Shortly afterward I began to see Vivian, and then her boyfriend, Boyd Fiske, everywhere we went. When

I saw them in a parked car across the street from the playground when I came to pick up you and Emma, I knew that we all had to disappear, and that was when I began to make plans to move to the West Coast.

I received a written death threat, the day of our wedding. When we came back from Maine I encountered Boyd Fiske outside my office. I confronted him and offered to pay him to take Vivian away from us.

Boyd informed me that Vivian hated me and wanted revenge and had talked about killing me, my grandmother and my daughter. He said she had become particularly insensed when she saw the announcement of our wedding.

Again, Sarah, I considered going to the police, but again couldn't bear to have it all made public. Boyd assured me he could keep Vivian in check if I gave him ten thousand dollars, which I did. That bought us a couple of weeks of peace before the calls started again. After that there were more payments, more broken promises, and I knew they would never end.

I finally confronted Vivian and told her I was going to the police. She laughed and said, "Go ahead—and I'll tell them you hired me to kill Tamara, and I'm sure they'll check and find out you gave me five thousand dollars the day after she died, not to mention a couple of incriminating letters you wrote." Sarah, I did give her the money—it was money I had earlier collected for her psychiatric treatment that I didn't feel right keeping. The letters…well, you know how words can be twisted.

Anyway, I could see that she might very well present enough circumstantial evidence to implicate me in Tamara's death. How could I allow that to happen?

What would it have done to Emma? I simply didn't dare go to the police.

So I hired Meredith and Parker to watch you, Emma and my grandmother, twenty-four hours a day, while I flew out here to find a place to live where I hoped Vivian would not find us. They also had a tail on Vivian. But almost immediately the investigators informed me that they had lost track of her.

Tonight I am setting all of these facts down in this letter to you Sarah because Vivian Novak is here in Emerald Cove. She showed up at Cliff House this evening, driving a Mercedes.

I don't know where Boyd is, but I'm sure he's not far away.

Sarah, I tried to cover my tracks, I don't know how she found me, but I do know this woman, although twisted, is brilliantly clever and cunning. Don't underestimate her.

I realize now I should have gone to the police in the very beginning. Now it's too late. What proof do I have? Besides, the Emerald Cove Police Department consists of a handful of officers; even if I could convince them she is dangerous, I can't expect them to protect us. We have to disappear. There's no other way.

Since you and Emma and my grandmother are due to arrive the day after tomorrow, I am trying to buy time. I spoke to the owner of a yacht today. He wants to sell it but may agree to a charter to take us to Mexico as soon as you arrive.

I have offered Vivian another ten thousand dollars. I pretended I would have to get the money from the bank. Actually I brought cash with me because I didn't want to make a bank transfer that possibly could be traced. The money is hidden in the attic in a shoe box.

I have promised Vivian I will get the money for her tomorrow, but intend to stall until you arrive and we can sail for Mexico. Just in case anything goes wrong, however, I am going to ask Meredith and Parker to keep this letter for you.

After speaking with Vivian tonight, I am convinced she is criminally insane.

Regretfully,
Mark

Chapter Twenty-One

The accompanying report from Meredith and Parker for the most part detailed the surveillance they had performed, painstakingly listing the various locations and movements of the people involved.

Sarah and Ben skimmed through it quickly.

Near the end of the report it was noted that their investigator had again picked up the trail of Vivian Novak and that she and Boyd Fiske had bought airline tickets to Las Vegas. There was an added notation to the effect that Boyd was known to have frequented the Atlantic City casinos.

"Bingo!" Ben murmured.

Sarah leaned back in her chair, her mind racing. "So Meredith and Parker didn't warn Mark they were en route to Vegas because they figured Boyd and Vivian were just going to gamble, probably with the ten thousand Mark had already given them."

"The P.I.'s told you a full report had already been sent out here, remember? This is a duplicate. They probably felt they had given Mark the information about Vivian's whereabouts. He hadn't had a phone installed, so they couldn't call. Since you didn't find their first report, it was either lost in the mail, which is unlikely, or Vivian got her hands on it."

Sarah nodded, and picked up the last page of the report. "Ben, look at this. There's a postscript. 'We have just learned via one of our connections that Vivian Novak hired a skip tracer to track down Dr. Mark Lasiter on the same day he departed from Kennedy.'"

Ben said, "What probably happened is that Vivian hired the skip tracer, then took off on the gambling trip with Boyd. While she's in Vegas, the skip tracer calls and tells her Mark is here on the coast. Maybe Boyd has already gambled away all their money and they don't have air fare. So they decide to hitchhike—"

"And run into the unfortunate Mae Peterson," Sarah finished for him.

"With this report, your husband's letter and the broker's description of the real Mae Peterson . . . we've got her now, Sarah," Ben said.

"But we don't have Emma and Harriet. What if the police show up and spook her before they find them?"

Ben drummed his fingers on the table thoughtfully. "They haven't exactly been helpful so far. Besides which, Elliot even sees you as a suspect, so you've got a point. I've got to go into town and start questioning everybody—anybody who might have seen them."

"You know, Ben," Sarah said slowly, "I keep thinking about that house on Dolphin Drive that Mae—Vivian rented. There was a small attached garage. At least one of the cars that were parked on the driveway, the Mercedes or the Porsche, could have been parked inside. With all the rain we've been having, wouldn't you have preferred to get to your car from the house, rather than dashing across a driveway in the pouring rain?"

"You think she might be holding Harriet and Emma in the garage?"

"I don't know. But if they were in the house, as loudly as we spoke, they would surely have heard us. Unless they were gagged they would have called out to us. But if they were in the garage . . ."

"It's a long shot, but worth investigating. With this weather, it's going to be dark early this afternoon. As soon as it is I'm going to get into that garage."

"What if Elliot comes back to question me further, or even brings a warrant for my arrest? I'll have to give him the report and the letter and tell him everything. I hope withholding the information is the right thing to do. I just think we need to know where Emma and Harriet are before we involve him. At this point, he might even decide to arrest me for Mark's death—and then only you would be left to search for Harriet and Emma."

"I can hardly break into the garage in broad daylight. We'll just have to stay out of the cops' way until it's dark," Ben said. "We'll eat, then drive to town. There are a few people who pretty much know everything that goes on in town that I can question."

"Ben, I just thought of something else. The saltwater taffy Mae brought. I threw it in the trash, but I remember it was in a paper bag that had Neptune's Candy Store, Sandy Point printed on the outside. Where is Sandy Point?"

"About ten miles south. More of a tourist town than Emerald Cove because it has a nice sandy beach."

"Perhaps we could drive down there and see if anyone remembers Mae, and if she had a child or an elderly lady with her."

"Sure, it's worth a shot. And it will keep us out of the way of the Emerald Cove PD."

AFTER A FEW FITFUL HOURS without rain, the storm returned in all its fury midafternoon. Thunder roared down the coast, lightning split the sky, and the rain came down in a solid sheet.

They had spent a disappointing morning. No one Ben questioned in town had seen Harriet and Emma—with Vivian or Boyd, or anyone else. The drive to Sandy Point had also proved fruitless.

When the storm broke, Ben drove Sarah back to his house.

"Get out of those wet clothes and take a warm bath," he instructed. "With the cloud cover, it's going to be pitch dark soon. I'll go to Dolphin Drive. You can wait here. Keep the doors locked and don't answer the bell until I come back."

"I'd rather change clothes and go with you."

"They're less likely to spot me if I'm alone. Let me do this, Sarah."

"All right. But if you're not back in—"

"Give me a couple of hours. By the time I've driven into town and maybe hung around waiting for an opportunity, I'll need at least that long. I'll call you if I have anything to report. Don't pick up the phone, let the answering machine get it."

The moment Ben departed, Sarah regretted not going with him. She took a hot shower, and was donning dry clothes when Ben's telephone rang. He had been gone only minutes. Sarah ran down the stairs and reached the living room just as the machine picked up.

Her skin crawled as Mae—Vivian's voice purred, "Hey, Sarah, I know you're there. Listen . . . maybe you should come home to Cliff House."

There was a pause, then a child's frightened voice spoke. "Please, Sarah."

Emma!

Sarah snatched up the phone in time to hear Mae whisper, "I'll see the cops coming a mile off, hon. By the time they get here, no telling what they'll find. And I'll be long gone."

"Mae—" Sarah screamed, but the line had gone dead. She punched 911 and shifted impatiently from one foot to the other until the emergency operator answered. "This is Mrs. Lasiter—I just had a call from the woman who kidnapped Emma—what? She's four years old. You already have a report. Please, send officers to Cliff House immediately. I'm going there now."

Sarah slammed down the phone and raced back upstairs, pulled on her boots, grabbed her coat and car keys and stumbled back down the stairs. Knowing the police response time was at least fifteen minutes under the best weather conditions, she knew she couldn't wait for them. She had to get to Emma right away.

Grabbing a poncho from the coatrack, she pulled it over her head and raced outside. The wind took her breath away. Driving up the hill, she wished she had not put the money in the bank. Perhaps waving the cash at Vivian would have mollified her sufficiently that she would have let them leave. Was Harriet with them?

Was Boyd?

Sarah didn't dare think about confronting him. The main thing was, Emma was all right and they would be reunited soon. She'd worry about the rest later.

Pulling into the driveway at Cliff House, Sarah peered through the rain-splashed windshield but could see no sign of lights anywhere in the house. She dashed from the car to the house, breathlessly fumbling with the key before realizing the front door was ajar.

Stepping into the hall, she called out, "Mae? Where are you?"

There was no response.

There was a puddle of rain on the floor and the house was as cold as the rainswept night. Reaching for the light switch, Sarah flipped it up and down but nothing happened.

"Damn," she muttered under her breath. The fuse box was outside. She called again, "Mae! It's me, Sarah."

Still no answer.

She tried to remember where she had put the flashlight. In the kitchen?

Why didn't Mae respond? Was it possible she had left? Could Emma be here, all alone and terrified?

Feeling her way carefully across the hall to the kitchen door, she paused to get her bearings. A strong, gamy odor assailed her.

Clapping her hand over her mouth and nose, she groped along the counters. A drawer near the sink contained miscellaneous items. There should be a flashlight, or at least candles, there. But the room was pitch dark and almost immediately she stumbled over something lying on the floor.

Gasping in fright, she nudged it with her foot. The thing on the floor seemed to be both rigid and yielding at the same time. Biting back a scream, she fell to her knees, fearing that she was about to find Emma's lifeless body.

In the darkness her hands touched something bristly, then her searching fingers found a sticky mass of pulpy, raw flesh. Jerking away her hands, she fell backward in her haste to get away from the thing on the floor. Whatever it was, at least it wasn't a child.

She clambered to her feet and staggered out of the kitchen. Halfway across the hall she tripped and went sprawling on the wet floor. The house surrounded her, enclosed her. She felt trapped, panicked.

Get a grip, Sarah. Slowly and deliberately she climbed to her feet and found her way to the front door. In the wet darkness it was difficult to see the fuse box without a flashlight, and she circled the house twice before finding it. Precious minutes were ticking away. She daren't imagine what else she might find inside the house. She yanked on the fuse switches, pulling everything in the box.

Instantly light beamed from the balcony over her head. She raced back to the front door, her breath grinding painfully in her chest, and paused on the threshold.

Still silent, the house seemed to wait malevolently.

She flipped on the hall light, walked slowly toward the kitchen, then reached around the door and switched on the light.

There was a dead animal lying on the floor. It looked like a small dog, and she hastily averted her eyes.

She looked around the kitchen. Nothing seemed out of place.

She walked cautiously up the stairs to the living room, then checked the captain's mess. All appeared to be in order.

All right, Mae I know you're trying to scare me, but damn you, you're not going to succeed. She mounted the stairs to the third floor, every nerve in her body alert to every creak and groan the rain-soaked house made.

A quick check of the master bedroom yielded nothing, and Harriet's bedroom was also in order. Sarah closed her eyes and uttered a quick prayer before proceeding to Emma's room. Pushing open the door, she tried the light switch. Nothing happened. The light from the landing painted a dim path across the child's bed.

Mr. Buttons, a knife through his chest, was pinned to Emma's pillow.

Chapter Twenty-Two

Sarah drove down the hill like a madwoman, anger boiling inside her as the rental car hurtled around the curves of the treacherous cliff road.

On the passenger seat beside her lay Emma's teddy bear. Mr. Buttons' stuffing oozed from the jagged tear in his belly where the knife had pinned him to the pillow.

She had pulled out the knife, grabbed Mr. Buttons, and half run, half fallen down the stairs. Slamming the front door behind her, she didn't bother to lock it. Vivian or Boyd or both were not stopped by locked doors, so why bother?

Sarah's rage propelled her down the hill with no clear idea of where she intended to go or what she intended to do. Just past Ben's house she met the patrol car responding to her call.

As she braked and flashed her lights at the officers, several things occurred to her. All she could show them was the body of the dog. The police believed Harriet had taken Emma away and wanted a restraining order to keep her away from them. To the police, she was not only an abuser, but also possibly a murderer.

One of the officers left the patrol car and approached as Sarah rolled down her window. "I'm sorry—I shouldn't have panicked. It was another prank call. I do have proof, though—on Mr. Travis's answering machine, if you'd care to hear it.''

Rain dripped from the officer's hat. ''I don't think that'll be necessary.'' He turned without another word and went back to the patrol car. Sarah waited until they made a U-turn and drove down the hill, then she followed, knowing now what her destination would be. She drove straight to Dolphin Drive and parked on the corner of the street.

The street lamps were amber orbs behind a veil of rain. There were a few cars parked on the street, but no sign of Ben's minivan. Had he come and gone? Or could he at this very minute be trying to get into their garage?

Sarah decided she couldn't wait to find out. She had to confront Vivian and demand that she release Emma. The phone call, of course, had not been made from Cliff House. They had already been in the house, left the dead animal, stabbed Mr. Buttons, then left to make the phone call from somewhere else. Vivian was evidently not finished torturing her yet.

Turning the key in the ignition again, Sarah started the car and drove along the street, stopping in front of the rented house. The lights were on and again the harsh sound of a heavy metal group blared. Sarah rang the bell and hammered on the door at the same time.

Boyd flung open the door. ''What the hell—'' He swayed slightly on his feet. Sarah had seen enough addicts while working for Mark to recognize the dilated pupils and glazed stare.

''Where is she?'' Sarah demanded, pushing past him into the house, feeling drunk with anger and recklessness. ''What have you done with Emma?''

Vivian uncoiled herself from the couch, a cigarette drooping from her mouth. She wore the same pink satin robe and her feet were bare, wads of cotton between her toes. Several bottles of nail polish on the coffee table jostled for space with take-out cartons from a chicken franchise and beer cans. Unlike Boyd, Vivian did not appear to be under the influence of either drugs or alcohol.

She turned off the music and regarded Sarah with malicious satisfaction. "So you lost his kid, did you? What makes you think she's here?"

"Your phone call. Where is Emma? I know you have her. Harriet, too."

Boyd walked unsteadily back to the couch and collapsed. "What phone call?"

Ignoring him, Sarah addressed Vivian, "You called me and said Emma was at Cliff House."

Vivian shrugged. "Not me. Maybe it was the old lady?"

"It was you—" Sarah had been about to call her Vivian, but stopped herself in time. *Better not give away I'm aware of her identity, not yet.* "I don't know what you want from me, but please, let me take Emma and Harriet with me now."

Vivian's attitude underwent an abrupt change, from spiteful nonchalance to pouting rage. "You moved right in, didn't you? Thought you'd just take over. Rich husband, ready-made family. Who the hell gave you the right to *just move in?*" Her voice dropped venomously.

Boyd seemed to rouse himself. "Mae," he warned, then, as if to drive home his point, he repeated, *"Mae."*

"You knew my husband, didn't you?" Sarah said. "From where? To my knowledge he was never in Las Vegas."

"I met him here, in Emerald Cove, before you chased him down," Vivian said. "He told me he was trying to dump you."

"That's not true. Nothing you've told me is true. I'm going to the police. I've got your voice and Emma's voice on Ben Travis's answering machine."

Vivian and Boyd exchanged grins, eroding Sarah's confidence that the message on the machine would still be there. For the first time she noticed that Boyd's hair was wet and there was mud on his boots, testifying to the fact that he had recently been outside. What was the relationship between the two? she wondered. If they were more than partners in crime, why did Boyd tolerate Mae-Vivian's obsession with Mark? Was it for money?

"You're imagining things, babe," Boyd said. "Guess it's time for us to call the cops and tell them you came busting in here like a crazy woman, accusing this poor bereaved widow of all sorts of crimes. You know what, Mae, between suing the shrink's estate for wrongful death for Henry and...let's see, defamation of character, maybe? We could be on easy street for quite a while."

"Is that what you want?" Sarah asked. "Money? If you let me take Emma and Harriet home now, I promise I will get ten thousand dollars for you tomorrow. That's all I have in the world and I don't know how I'm going to be able to pay Mark's hospital bills, but I'll gladly give it to you—"

Vivian's grin widened. "You've really cracked up, haven't you, hon? Guess you lost your marbles in the fire that burned up your folks and your boyfriend about a year ago, huh? I mean, that was how you hooked the doc, right? You were his patient after you cracked up. I hear he liked to get it on with his patients."

Sarah felt some of her blind anger turn to caution. Vivian had done her homework. Mark's words of warning came back. *Don't underestimate her.*

"Hey, think of the lawsuits if that comes out," Boyd said slyly. "Him getting it on with patients."

"I bet your insurance company would like to know about that fire you were in back East," Vivian said. "You know, in view of your garage up on the cliff burning up."

Sarah felt a sudden urge to fly at the woman with flailing fists. Instead, she drew a deep breath and screamed at the top of her lungs, "Emma! Harriet! Are you here? It's me, Sarah."

That galvanized Boyd into action. He leapt from the couch and came toward her, his expression ugly. "Why, you—"

The peril of her situation finally dawned on Sarah and she turned and stumbled to the door. She had just yanked it open when she felt Boyd's hands on her arms, spinning her around. Behind him Vivian was yelling something unintelligible.

A quiet voice cut through the din of the shouts and the storm. "Let her go."

Ben stepped forward into the light.

Startled, Boyd let go of Sarah and swung wildly at Ben, who neatly sidestepped, causing Boyd to plunge out onto the porch. Ben quickly moved between Boyd and Sarah, seized Sarah's arm and gave her a slight push. "Go on, get out of here, now."

Sarah ran for her car, parked at the gate. She flung herself behind the wheel and started the engine, then reached across the passenger seat and opened the door.

In the light emitted from the house she saw Boyd lunge toward Ben, who again moved swiftly out of range. But Boyd recovered quickly and Sarah gasped as she saw a huge fist swing toward Ben's face.

Ducking, Ben jabbed with a left hook that connected with Boyd's jaw and sent him reeling. Taking advantage of the split second while Boyd was spinning in an uncertain circle, Ben raced down the driveway.

Sarah held her breath, hoping whatever substance had Boyd under its influence would slow his reflexes. She realized now how foolhardy she had been, placing herself and Ben in danger.

Ben ran across the lawn and vaulted over the fence. The instant he was in her car she floored the accelerator and the car skidded forward.

"Take it easy, Sarah," Ben warned breathlessly. "No need to attract the attention of a patrol car. Boyd is too stewed to come after us and besides, Mae was yelling at him to let you go."

Sarah eased up on the accelerator. "I'm sorry, Ben. I didn't know you were still there. I put you in danger."

"Why on earth did you come after me?"

"I'll explain in a minute. Did you get a look in the garage?"

"Sure did. There's a back door and it was unlocked. Nothing in there but broken-down furniture and various other junk, crammed in wall-to-wall. I could hear that godawful music playing inside the house and the Porsche was gone. I was wondering if I could find an unlocked window and get inside, when Boyd came back. So I hung around, hoping maybe they'd both leave. Then I saw the lights were on in a house across the street, so I decided I'd see if the neighbors had seen anything suspicious. A nice old couple invited me in out of the rain."

"Had they seen Emma or Harriet?" Sarah asked eagerly.

"Afraid not. Make a couple of left turns and take me back to my van. I left it on Marina Drive, which runs parallel to Dolphin. And I'd appreciate hearing now why you went barging in there when you knew I was in the midst of my covert operation."

SARAH LET OUT HER BREATH in a sigh of frustration as Ben patiently explained, "You picked up the phone while they were still on the line, before the beep. The message didn't record."

"It was Mae—Vivian. And Emma. I'm sure. The police wouldn't believe me anyway, so I suppose it doesn't matter."

"Stay here, Sarah. I'll go and check Cliff House. Have you got the key?"

"You won't need it." Sarah sighed. "I didn't lock the door."

Ben picked up the torn and now damp Mr. Buttons and handed the bear to her. "There's a sewing kit in the top left kitchen drawer. Why don't you do a little mending? You wouldn't want Emma to see Mr. Buttons like this."

She was glad to give her hands something to do. Time was running out and she was no closer to learning where Emma and Harriet were than before. How soon would it be before Detective Elliot arrived with a warrant for her arrest?

After stitching up Mr. Buttons, Sarah set the teddy bear beside the fire to dry. She glanced at the mantelpiece clock. Ben had been gone for twenty minutes. She went into the kitchen and put the kettle on. When the kettle boiled Sarah turned it off. She looked at the telephone, wondering whether to call Cliff House. Should she drive up there?

She was considering the two options when Ben's key turned in the lock. She ran to meet him. His hair was plastered to his head and his jacket was soaking wet.

"The dead animal wasn't a dog, it was a coyote, and it was roadkill," Ben said, peeling off his jacket and shaking raindrops from his hair. "I took it out of the house. I'll bury it tomorrow. Sarah, I put a new lock on the front door, remember? I checked all the French doors again and there's no sign any were jimmied, so there's got to be another way into the house. Call Cap'n Vaughan and ask him. I'm going to get dry clothes.''

The old man's phone rang thirteen times and Sarah finally hung up. She turned the kettle on again and paced nervously around the kitchen, then she went into the living room. Mr. Buttons regarded her reproachfully from his warm spot on the hearth. Sarah picked up the bear and held him close to her heart. She whispered, ''Oh, Emma, stay strong. I'm going to find you. I don't know how, but I swear I will.''

Ben returned, now dressed in dry clothes. ''Did you get Cap'n Vaughan?''

''No answer. He must be out.''

Ben picked up the phone and dialed information. ''I'll try the retirement community clubhouse, he may be there. I'd like to know how they got inside Cliff House tonight.''

He asked for the number and a moment later covered the receiver with his hand and said, ''They're having a ninetieth birthday party there tonight. They're paging the cap'n for me now... Hello? Oh, hi, Cap'n Vaughan. Ben Travis. *Travis*—your neighbor up on the hill. Yeah. Listen, Cap'n, we've got a real problem up here. Somebody's been breaking into Cliff House. I changed the locks and they still got in . . . you got any idea how that could happen?''

Sarah heard the muffled rasp of the old man's answer and then Ben said, ''No, no, it's not your fault. I understand. Okay, thanks.''

Ben looked at Sarah. ''The builder of that monstrosity was evidently fond of trapdoors. There's another one in the floor of the pantry—it's reached by a crawl space under the ground floor deck near the kitchen. Vaughan says he told everyone who was interested in the house about it, including your husband.''

"I never went into the pantry because it needed cleaning and I didn't have time to stock it. It's a big walk-in off the kitchen." Sarah shivered. "To think they could come and go, even when we were in the house!"

"Well, you're not going back there, so don't worry about it. Now I'm going to throw another log on the fire and we're going to toast our toes and get warm and relax. There's nothing more we can do tonight."

"I'll make some hot chocolate," Sarah said, not questioning the assumption that she would be spending the night. She certainly had no intention of going back to Cliff House.

When Sarah returned to the living room with the hot chocolate, Ben was standing in front of a roaring fire. As he took the steaming cup from her his hand grazed hers and she felt a jolt of awareness. She didn't dare look into his eyes.

Ben took one of the armchairs flanking the fireplace and, taking a cue from him, she took the other. The space between them seemed to resonate with longing.

For a moment they listened to the wind howling and the rain's staccato rhythm against the windows, then Ben said, "I must admit that weather like this makes me think of heading south. My father still has the old family home. It's right on the beach just north of San Diego. My folks bought it years ago before the price of beach property went out of sight."

He was trying to distract her, she knew. Not only from the horrors plaguing her, but also from their growing attraction. He surely must sense how she ached to crawl into his arms and nestle close, shutting out everything but the comfort of his body connected to hers.

She didn't trust herself to speak, for fear of revealing her emotions. Her own sense of honor forbade such feelings so soon after her husband's death, even though Mark had betrayed her trust and, it seemed, had married her for reasons other than love. She also knew instinctively that Ben's own integrity kept him on the far side of the fireplace, only occasionally allowing his eyes to search her face and send the unspoken message that he also hungered for her touch.

After a while Sarah closed her eyes and leaned back in her chair, the warmth of the fire and Ben's soothing conversation making her feel relaxed and drowsy in spite of her tension.

SARAH AWOKE with a start to the sound of the telephone ringing. She was lying on the couch covered by Ben's mother's shawl and her shoes had been removed. The fire had burned down to an ash-fringed mound of embers emitting only enough light for her to see Ben grab the phone.

He spoke softly. "Hello, yes, this is Ben Travis."

There was a long pause, then he said, "What happened? Was it a heart attack? Yes, yes, I understand. Where is he? Yes, I know where that is. I'll be there as soon as I can. I may not be able to get a flight down there tonight.... Yes, I understand that, and I will leave right away. Please do everything you can."

Sarah heard the phone drop into its cradle. She could see that Ben was standing motionless, his back turned to her, his hand still resting on the phone, and even in the dim light the tension in his shoulders was obvious.

"Ben, what is it? What happened?" she asked.

Turning, he flipped on a lamp. "My father...he's in the hospital," he said in a shocked voice. "They suspect a stroke..."

She asked quickly, "What can I do? Can I call the airlines while you pack?"

"I'm thinking that by the time I drive to the airport and then wait for a flight I could be halfway to San Diego on the freeway. If I drive all night, I can be there first thing in the morning. But, Sarah, I can't leave you here alone."

"You have to, Ben. I can't leave until I know what happened to Emma and Harriet."

Ben crossed the room and she rose from the couch. They went into each other's arms wordlessly.

Ben's grip tightened protectively around her. "Mae— Vivian called you here, at my number. Sarah, I'm not comfortable leaving you here alone. I think you should go to the police tonight, now. Tell them everything, and show them your husband's letter and the report from the investigators. After that you can spend the night in town at the hotel or the B-and-B. If Elliot decides all the proof is a hoax and arrests you, you'll still be safe. If you need to get in here for any reason, there's a key in the plant pot by the front door. But please don't come up the hill alone."

She knew by the tone of his voice that it would be useless to argue, even though she wasn't sure she wanted to go to the police yet, for fear of precipitating some action by Vivian or Boyd that could harm Emma and Harriet. Still, for now her main concern had to be getting Ben on his way without worrying about her. She said, "Yes, all right. I'll go to the police and then get a room in town."

Ben released her, tipping her face upward with his finger to look into her eyes. "I'll drive you to the police and the B-and-B before I leave."

"No…that will waste time. Besides, I'll need my own car to get around town."

"Okay, but I have to see you get to town safely. We'll leave here together."

"Go and pack, Ben. I'll make you a thermos of coffee."

Chapter Twenty-Three

Ben followed Sarah to the police station on Main Street and pulled into the parking slot beside her. Jumping out of her car as Ben opened his door, she said, "No need to come in with me, Ben. Just get on your way."

"Are you sure?"

"Yes. Go. I hope your father will be all right."

Returning to her car, she picked up the bulky envelope containing the investigators' reports.

The desk sergeant looked up as she entered the station. There was little activity and she could see only a dispatcher on duty with him. He evidently recognized her. "What can I do for you, Mrs. Lasiter?"

She placed the envelope on the desk. "These are reports from private investigators my husband hired. There is also a letter from my husband, explaining everything. I'm sure that the woman mentioned in here now calls herself Mae Peterson and that she is holding my husband's grandmother and his daughter against their will. We must act quickly to prevent her harming them."

The sergeant glanced at the clock on the wall beside him. It was nearly midnight. "Detective Elliot is handling the case, Mrs. Lasiter. He isn't here now. I'll see he gets this first thing in the morning."

"But this can't wait until morning. Can you get a search warrant and come with me to Mrs. Peterson's house tonight?"

The sergeant gave her an incredulous look. "No, ma'am. I can't. This isn't the NYPD. I'll give this report to Detective Elliot in the morning."

"Sergeant, this is a matter of life and death. At least call Detective Elliot and tell him what I have here."

The sergeant rolled his eyes and picked up the phone. A moment later he said, "I've got Mrs. Lasiter here. She *claims* she's got *more* evidence against Mrs. Peterson."

If he had held up his fingers to indicate derisive quote marks, Sarah thought, he could not have more effectively trivialized the statement. She glared at him as he added, "Yeah, okay. I'll tell her."

"Mrs. Lasiter, like I said, he'll read this material in the morning. Right now he has other things to do. Yours isn't the only case he's working on, y'know."

Gritting her teeth to keep from saying what was on her mind, Sarah strode to the door and, angry, stumbled on the wet steps outside. Regaining her balance, she forced herself to proceed more carefully to her car.

The streets were deserted and, feeling like the last living creature on earth, she drove slowly through town, making and discarding plans. The wildest of these was that she would acquire a weapon of some sort and confront Vivian, forcing her to divulge what she had done with Emma and Harriet. But Sarah quickly realized that she was incapable of interrogating her in any way that might get results, and besides, that would simply play into the psychopathic woman's hands.

What if she were to go to the elderly couple on Dolphin Street who lived opposite Vivian and Boyd and ask if she could rent a room from them? She could watch until both kidnappers left the house and then somehow break in. Harriet and Emma had to be there. They could not have disappeared without a trace. But that would be too time-consuming and time was not on her side. Detective Elliot was no doubt accumulating circumstantial evidence that she had killed Mark and could at any moment appear with a warrant for her arrest.

Almost without thinking, Sarah headed back to Dolphin Drive. The rain had dwindled to a misty drizzle and all of the houses were dark, including Vivian's. Trash cans now stood at the curb like sentinels in front of each house. awaiting pickup by the disposal company the following morning.

Parking in front of Vivian's house, Sarah stared at the trash can. Easing open the car door, she stepped out, careful not to slam the door behind her. The nearest streetlight stood in front of the house next door, emitting only a dim amber glow. She regretted not bringing a flashlight.

Lifting the heavy plastic lid of the trash can, Sarah clenched her nostrils against the stench and peered inside. The contents seemed to consist mostly of empty beer cans and discarded fast-food cartons. Pushing aside the top layer, she winced as the cans rattled.

She glanced over her shoulder at the house, but there was no sign of light or movement. Both the Mercedes and the Porsche were parked on the driveway. There was nothing in the top layer of trash that indicated the presence of Harriet and Emma in the house. Sarah wasn't even sure what she was looking for.

She scrutinized the cars parked on the driveway again. They were probably locked. Or were they? She glanced at the house. It was still dark and quiet.

There was a little more light on the driveway and Sarah crept around to the far side of the cars so that she was between them and the house next door. The houses were divided by a chain-link fence lined with a row of oleanders.

Both cars were locked. The windows were rain-spotted and although she pressed her face against the glass to look inside, she could see nothing but darkness.

Then, as suddenly as a scream, the porch light came on.

Sarah flung herself back into the oleanders, colliding with the chain-link fence.

Almost at once, the porch light was extinguished and she heard the front door open and Vivian's harsh whisper, "That was pretty stupid."

Boyd's voice responded sheepishly, "Hey, hon, I didn't think. I just automatically switched it on."

There was a pause, then Boyd muttered, "Come on, old woman, and remember, one peep out of you and I'll choke the life out of the kid here and now."

Harriet and Emma! Sarah pressed herself close to the wet earth, feeling the fence against her back and the dripping leaves of an oleander in her face. She felt terrified, yet relieved. They were bringing Emma and Harriet out and at least they were alive. Sarah wanted to rush forward and gather the child into her arms, but Boyd's chilling warning resounded in her ears.

She could see shadowy figures coming toward the parked cars. Boyd was first. He was carrying Emma and had his hand over her mouth. Behind him Harriet stumbled as Vivian pushed her forward.

Sarah wanted to scream and shout, but realized immediately that would be foolish since she couldn't be sure anyone would hear. Even if they did, they wouldn't necessarily come to her aid. No, she couldn't risk Emma being hurt, and she certainly couldn't tackle the burly Boyd on her own.

"Hey, look—" Vivian's voice spoke. "The car she drove is still parked in front."

Sarah held her breath.

Boyd said, "Travis must've taken her in his van."

"I could've sworn they went in her car."

"Well, you were wrong. Get in and let's get moving."

A car door whined open.

"One thing," Vivian said, "with him gone and her car here, that means she's up on the hill without wheels."

Sarah stiffened. *With him gone...* His father hadn't had a stroke! They'd wanted Ben out of the way. Sarah thought of Ben driving all night, and his anguish as he worried about how his father was faring, only to find out it was all a trick. But maybe he'd guess. Given all that had happened, *she* should have. Ben had been so shocked by the news he hadn't even questioned it.

There was a scuffling of feet and other car doors opened. The interior light of the Mercedes came on. Doors were closed quietly, and the engine started. The car glided out of the driveway and onto the street.

When it was almost out of sight, Sarah ran to her car. How closely dare she follow? With no traffic on the streets they would surely see and recognize her and then what would happen to their hostages? But she couldn't risk losing them again, either.

They turned right at the corner. She started her engine without turning on the headlights, waited a moment, then followed. Making the turn, she was just in time to see the taillights of the Mercedes disappear around another corner.

Driving without lights was frightening, especially with the misty rain obscuring her view, but she decided it was the only way to keep them in sight without being seen. Even without lights it was necessary to stay well behind them.

They led her to the Coast Highway and she was glad to see that there was some movement of traffic. Now she was able to keep a couple of vehicles between them, but close the distance slightly. She searched passing traffic in vain for a patrol car.

When the Mercedes turned up the old Cliff Road, Sarah had no doubt where they were going and she dropped back. What were they up to? How could anyone predict the actions of a psychopath? Or of the paroled killer she held under her spell?

Sarah was now proceeding at a snail's pace, nervous about the treacherous turns on the steep road at the best of times, even more so in the dark without headlights.

Reaching Ben's house, she turned into his driveway and braked. The Mercedes had gone on up the hill. From here she would proceed on foot. They mustn't know she was following. The biggest risk would be to precipitate some action that might get Emma or Harriet hurt. But first she had to call 911.

She ran into the house and flipped on the light switch. Nothing happened. She felt her way to the living room phone. There was no dial tone. Stumbling into the kitchen, she found the wall phone, but it, too, was dead, as were the lights.

The storm—or Sarah's stalkers—must have taken out both the phone and power lines. That meant Cliff House probably was also without electricity or phones. She was on her own. She would have to somehow get Emma and Harriet out of the house by stealth, since there was no one to come to her aid.

Oh, Ben, I wish you were here. For an instant, she wondered if she'd ever see him again. Rummaging through the kitchen drawers, she found a flashlight, checked it to be sure the battery wasn't dead, and went outside.

Walking up the steep grade, her breath soon began to grind in her chest. She wished she knew what they were planning to do. The only possibility that occurred to her, and which sent her running despite the pain in her chest, was that Vivian intended to kill them in Cliff House, thereby implicating her. Was this to be Vivian's revenge against the woman she believed had usurped her position in Marks' life? If she had kidnapped Emma and Harriet for ransom wouldn't she have demanded money? Or accepted Sarah's offer to pay her? No, this wasn't about ransom or extortion for Vivian. It was about revenge.

She had already killed Mark and probably the real Petersons, not to mention Mark's first wife. But Vivian wanted an even more satisfying punishment for Sarah. She wanted Sarah to be accused not only of murdering her husband, but also his daughter and grandmother. A death penalty case if ever there was one.

Cliff House loomed ahead, a dark tower against a night sky now intermittently split by shafts of moonlight as the rain clouds scudded east. The Mercedes was parked beside the gutted garage.

Sarah paused for a moment to catch her breath, then, flashlight in hand, approached the house. The front door appeared to be closed and presumably locked. She had her key, but using it would surely announce her arrival.

Circling the house, her gaze swept downward from the two upper balconies to the first-floor deck. The deck was about three feet above ground, supported by wooden posts. Sarah ducked underneath it.

Her flashlight found the opening into the house almost immediately. A square segment of the wooden wall enclosing the foundation had been removed and was lying on the ground. So much for a dead-bolted front door, she thought.

Putting aside thoughts of lurking rodents or hibernating snakes, she crouched to enter the small opening, and was about to turn on the flashlight when she heard voices, so close she was startled. She saw the trapdoor then, lying open no more than six feet away.

"One of them dragged the coyote carcass out of here." Vivian's voice floated down. "Hope it was her who found it. Hope she went up to the kid's room and saw what I left for her there."

"Find the damn matches, Viv. We haven't got all night."

Matches? Sarah prayed there really was a power outage and they were going to light candles.

Harriet spoke then, her voice tired but surprisingly strong. "You aren't going to get away with this. Please, there's still time to get away. Why don't you leave us here— you can tie us up again. You'll be gone before Sarah comes back and finds us."

Tie us up *again,* Sarah thought, her anger rising. So Harriet and Emma had been bound and probably gagged somewhere in the house on Dolphin Drive. Oh, to be Boyd's physical equal, for just a few minutes.

Whatever they were planning, it was imminent. Sarah didn't have time to think. She had to divert them in some way. She quickly backed out from under the house, picked up a rock and hurled it at the kitchen window. She heard the glass shatter and Boyd's voice, "What the hell—"

Sarah sprinted around the house to the front door and rang the bell, keeping her thumb on the button until she saw through the frosted window panel a flashlight beam crossing the hall.

Backing away, she picked up another rock. As the front door burst open, she hurled the rock and was gratified to hear a gasp of pain. Then Vivian screamed, "She's out here somewhere. Boyd, come and get her!"

Sarah ran back around to the deck, dove underneath and crawled to the trapdoor. A three-step ladder took her up through the pantry floor. Pushing open the door, she called softly, "Harriet, where are you?"

She could hear Boyd and Vivian shouting to each other in front of the house. Emma was whimpering nearby.

Boyd yelled, "I'm going around back! Watch the driveway!"

"Sarah! Is that you?" Harriet called. "We're here—in the kitchen, near the hall door."

Not daring to turn on her flashlight, Sarah went in the direction of Harriet's voice.

"Maybe she got inside the house," Vivian shouted, her voice coming from the deck.

Sarah collided with Emma in the darkness and bent to put her arms around the child. Never had human contact felt more wonderful.

She felt Harriet's hand on her arm. "Are you alone?"

"Yes. Quick, up the stairs, we can't get out without being seen. They've got both the back and the front covered." There was so much to say. Neither Harriet nor Emma knew of Mark's death—but there was no time.

Picking up the trembling little girl, Sarah ran up the staircase, with Harriet at her heels, just as Vivian shouted from the kitchen, "Get in here, Boyd. Now I can't find the old lady and the kid. They're hiding someplace."

Chapter Twenty-Four

Boyd's heavy footsteps hit the hall floor just as Sarah reached the second floor landing. When Harriet caught up with her Sarah whispered, "Emma's room."

They went up to the bedroom landing, huddling low as a flashlight beam swept the spiral staircase. In Emma's room Sarah closed the door, put Emma down, then switched on her flashlight. "It's all right, honey. I'm here now. I won't let them hurt you."

The chid regarded her with wide frightened eyes. Harriet, her eyes sunken and smudged with fatigue, looked older and more frail than ever.

Sarah picked up a chair and placed it under the trapdoor in the ceiling, she handed Harriet the flashlight and whispered, "There's an attic up there. I'll lift Emma up and then we're going to have to figure out how to get you up, too. If we both get on the chair, do you think I could boost you up?"

"I'll try," the older woman replied gamely.

Sarah stood on the chair and pushed open the trapdoor then Harriet lifted Emma into her arms.

"Emma, baby, I know it's dark up there, but Nana will be right behind you, okay?"

Emma nodded. Sarah hoisted the child up into the attic then turned and offered her hand to Harriet, moving aside slightly to make room for her on the chair.

Reaching upward, Harriet was able to grasp the trapdoor frame. Clasping her hands together, Sarah waited for Harriet to position her foot, then said, "Okay, on the count of three. Ready? One, two—"

"Three." She was surprised at how light Harriet was and knew she must be taking most of her weight on her arms. But they didn't achieve their goal the first try. A second determined attempt brought results. Sarah was able to raise Harriet high enough that with a final push she sprawled into the attic.

Seconds later, Harriet's face appeared, dust-streaked and triumphant. "Give my your hand, Sarah, I'll help you up."

"I'm not coming up. I'm going to try to lead them away from the house. Meantime, see if you can find some heavy object, a trunk or something, and drag it over the trapdoor."

Harriet didn't argue. She nodded. "Please be careful, Sarah. That woman hates us and Boyd is completely in her control."

"I wish I could leave the flashlight with you, but I'm going to need it."

"We'll be all right."

"Close the trapdoor now," Sarah whispered urgently.

She waited until the trapdoor was back in place and then removed the chair. She heard the scraping sound of something being dragged overhead.

Opening the bedroom door, Sarah listened.

Boyd's and Vivian's voices were raised in argument and sounded as if they were on the second floor, where the living areas, including the captain's mess, were located. There would be no way for her to get past them via the staircase without being seen and she needed a head start before giving away her position, to make them think Harriet and Emma were with her.

She tiptoed across the landing to the master bedroom, then made her way out onto the balcony. Oh, for a nice thick Pacific fog to roll in now! But as the storm moved east it was leaving clear skies in its wake and a half-moon painted the cliffs pale silver.

Descending the steps to the balcony below, Sarah crept toward the living room's French doors. Moonlight flooded the room, revealing no sign of either Boyd or Vivian.

Sarah's heart skipped. Had they gone up to the bedrooms? She had to divert them away from Emma's room, quickly.

She fumbled in her pocket for the key to the French doors, then discovered the doors were unlocked. Vivian and Boyd had no doubt already checked this balcony.

Stepping inside, Sarah heard Boyd's voice, somewhere below her. "I'm going out to get the car keys out of the ignition. I don't want them taking off in our car. We can run 'em down on foot if they get out. You check the bedrooms."

Boyd's heavy footsteps clumped down the stairs.

Sarah locked the French doors, then sped down the stairs after him. As soon as Boyd was outside, she closed the front door and locked it, then ran back into the pantry. She dropped the trapdoor back into place and wedged the pantry door shut with a kitchen chair. If she could keep Boyd outside long enough, perhaps she could deal with Vivian.

The doorbell rang, announcing Boyd's return. His muffled voice shouted something.

Vivian yelled, "All right, I'm coming."

Sarah grabbed a frying pan from the stove and silently moved to the door leading to the entry hall. She could see

Vivian's flashlight beam preceding her down the spiral staircase.

Boyd was still ringing the bell and pounding on the door.

Sarah waited until Vivian had almost reached the front door, then charged. She swung the frying pan at the shadowy figure and felt it connect with something solid. There was a startled cry, the flashlight flew from Vivian's hands, and she crumpled into a heap at Sarah's feet.

The doorbell stopped ringing. A second later something crashed against the frosted-glass panel of the front door. Sarah heard the glass crack with the impact. Boyd was going to smash his way in.

Stepping over Vivian's inert form, Sarah ran into the captain's mess and lifted the lid of the sea chest. Her fingers closed around the harpoon. It was heavier than she remembered.

A pulse pounded in her ears as she returned to the front door. The moonlight illuminated the hulking silhouette of Boyd. He had broken the frosted-glass panel and was reaching inside with one arm.

Sarah thought of Emma and Harriet, of the terror Boyd had inflicted upon them. Her hands trembled as she lifted the harpoon.

Seconds later Boyd unlocked the door and pushed it open. Sarah thrust the harpoon at him.

He bellowed with pain and the harpoon was yanked from her hands as he staggered backward onto the porch, the barbed tip of the weapon had embedded in his chest just below his shoulder.

Sarah raced up the spiral staircase to Emma's room.

"Harriet! It's me—open the trapdoor." She pulled a chair into position.

It seemed to take Harriet several minutes to remove whatever she had dragged over the trapdoor and open it.

"We have to get out of here—fast," Sarah said. "Hand Emma down to me, and then I'll help you."

Harriet didn't ask questions. The child was handed down and Sarah hugged her reassuringly, then placed her on the floor. "Okay, Harriet, now turn around and lower yourself through feet first. I'll grab your legs."

It was easier to help Harriet down than it had been to boost her up. When they were all safely on the floor Sarah said, "I knocked Vivian—Mae—out. She's unconscious. And I'm pretty sure I've disabled Boyd, too."

"Oh, my," Harriet said admiringly. "How resourceful of you."

"We're going to go downstairs now. Emma, I want you to hold on to Nana's hand. I'll go first."

But Emma was now rigid with shock, her eyes glazed.

Sarah pulled a blanket from the bed and wrapped it around the child. She was thinking rapidly that if by now Boyd had passed out she would try to relieve him of his car keys. It would be easier to drive down the hill than to walk carrying the little girl. She lifted Emma into her arms. "Okay, let's go."

Opening the bedroom door, she was instantly assailed by the acrid smell of smoke. At the same time a smoke detector shrieked its warning. Stepping out onto the landing, she saw flames leaping up the stairwell.

Sarah was paralyzed. For an instant she was immobilized, her mind whirling back to the hotel fire that had taken the lives of her parents and fiancé.

The flames illuminated Vivian, who was moving around at the bottom of the stairs. She held an object in her hand that looked like a gasoline can. She was screaming something, but Sarah couldn't make out the words over the roar of the fire.

Emma began to cough and choke on the smoke and Sarah reeled backward into the bedroom.

She tightened her grip on the child, but all at once she couldn't seem to move her feet, or even think.

Harriet grabbed her arm. "Sarah...they've set the house on fire, haven't they? We must get out."

Sarah nodded, but otherwise still couldn't move. A terrible sense of inevitability gripped her. Perhaps she had always been destined to perish in the flames. Perhaps she had only temporarily cheated death by fire when she escaped from the burning hotel.

Smoke was now creeping under the bedroom door.

"We have to get out!" Harriet said urgently. "Sarah, please, what shall we do?"

Emma made a small whimpering cry and Sarah looked down at the child's face. Emma's life had scarcely begun, and she didn't deserve to die. She mustn't die. Sarah knew she had to overcome her own fear and save the little girl.

"We can't get down the stairs," she said. "We'll have to get across the landing to the master bedroom and out onto the balcony."

Opening the door again, Sarah was appalled by the density of the smoke. The crackle of flames seemed much closer. Fearing Harriet might become disoriented or even overcome, Sarah said, "I'll lead the way, you hold on to my coat. We'd better crawl."

Holding Emma close, Sarah dropped to her knees, waited until she felt Harriet grab her coat, then crawled across the smoke-filled landing. Mercifully the master bedroom door had remained closed and there was little smoke in the room.

"Take Emma and wait for me on the balcony," Sarah said as she handed Emma to Harriet, "I'm going to knot some bedsheets."

As Harriet carried the child outside, Sarah closed the door and pulled a rug across the bottom of it. Feeling calmer now, she pulled two sheets from the bed, knotted the corners together, then went to the linen cupboard and grabbed two more sheets.

Once outside, Sarah tossed the two sheets to the balcony below, then she tied one end of the makeshift rope to the rail and dropped the other end over the side. "Harriet, you go first. You just have to get down to the next balcony. It isn't far. You can do it."

Harriet shook her head. She was trembling. "I can't, Sarah. You must save yourself and Emma."

"You've got to at least try, Harriet. Look, I'll pull the sheet back up and wrap and tie them around you. If you can't hold on, at least the sheets will stop you from falling to the ground."

"No! Sarah. I can't do it."

"Then we're all going to die, because I won't leave you," Sarah snapped. "Is that what you want?"

Tears stung Sarah's eyes as she spoke, only partially caused by the smoke. She hated having to speak to Harriet so harshly.

Wordlessly, Harriet reached for the bedsheets, climbed stiffly up onto the balcony rail, and lowered herself out of sight. Looking down, Sarah saw the fragile figure swing precariously for a moment, then Harriet's feet hit the lower balcony rail.

Way to go, Harriet, Sarah thought.

It took another minute for Harriet to ease herself down onto the balcony, then she shook the bedsheets and called up to them, "I'm down. You can come now."

"Emma, listen to me, baby," Sarah said. "You must help me now. You've got to put your arms around my neck and hold on real tight."

The child didn't respond. She was almost catatonic with shock. Sarah recognized that the little girl had been so traumatized that she had simply withdrawn into herself, shutting out everything and everyone else.

Hating herself even more, Sarah shook Emma slightly. "Come on, sweetheart, put your arms around my neck."

Smoke was now pouring into the bedroom. How long would it be before the flames reached the floor below and consumed the balcony where Harriet waited? They still had to climb down to the lower deck, and since Vivian had obviously recovered sufficiently to start the fire, she could well be waiting for them below. But the flames and smoke were a more immediate peril.

Sarah pulled up the bedsheets and wrapped them tightly around Emma, then around her own waist and shoulders. She needed to keep her hands free, but worried that Emma might slip away from her during the descent. Still, she had no choice.

As soon as she started over the rail Emma's arms went around her neck and she clung tightly during the brief drop to the balcony below. Handing the child to Harriet, Sarah swung over the rail and landed on her feet.

She saw then to her horror that the living room was ablaze. Flames were beginning to shoot through the outer walls. Black smoke now surrounded them.

"Sarah, the deck is on fire," Harriet said quietly. "We can't go down that way."

"All right—we'll go to the end of the balcony and drop down to the ground. It isn't much farther." She was busy knotting the other two sheets together as she spoke.

At the far end of the balcony Sarah began to tie the bedsheets to the rail, but she saw at once that there was now insufficient length to reach the ground. She had planned on going straight down, balcony to deck, but would now have to drop to the ground, which was at least three feet below the deck. She couldn't be sure because of the swirling smoke, but she estimated that there would be a drop of at least six feet. There was no way fragile eighty-year-old bones could stand the impact.

Closing her eyes, Sarah prayed as she had never prayed before. *I have to go first and then catch her.*

Trying not to communicate her fear, she said, "Harriet, I'll take Emma down first. Then I'll be able to catch you. Come down the minute you feel me give a couple of tugs on the sheets."

The descent was longer and more harrowing than before because of the smoke. At one point they smashed into the balcony supports and Sarah winced as pain shot through her knees.

"Hold on tight, Emma," she said into the child's ear. "We're nearly down."

She came to the end of the sheets and couldn't see the ground. *Please, don't let me fall on Emma.*

Then all at once Ben's voice came out of the smoky darkness. "Sarah! Sarah, where are you?"

"Here," she screamed. "At the north side of the house. Hurry!" She didn't know how or why, but by some miracle Ben was here and her heart rejoiced.

Seconds later she felt his hands on her ankles. "Okay, I've got you."

"I'm holding Emma. I'm afraid I'll drop her."

"Let go, Sarah. I'll catch both of you. Hurry, the whole house is engulfed."

There was a terrifying moment when she and the child seemed to hang in the smoke-filled air, then Ben's arms were around her and Emma cried out, "You're squishing me."

"Ben, Harriet's up there," Sarah said hoarsely.

He grabbed the sheets and started up without a word. Sarah had seen army rope climbers who would have been proud to climb aloft so swiftly. She marveled again at the strength of his arms and shoulders.

Placing Emma on the ground, she said, "Put the blanket over your mouth and nose, honey. I've got to help Nana now."

Minutes later when Ben swung down with Harriet clinging to him, Sarah grabbed Harriet's legs and they collapsed into a breathless heap.

Ben dropped to his feet and helped them up. "Let's get out of this smoke." He picked up Emma.

Sarah helped Harriet, who was limping.

"I thought you were on your way to San Diego," Sarah croaked to Ben, her throat raw from the smoke.

"I was half an hour down the freeway when I realized the call was probably a hoax. I called the hospital in San Diego on my cell phone. My father had not been admitted. I called him at home and he was fine."

They could hear sirens wailing up the hill.

"I called 911," Ben said. "I saw the fire from the bottom of the hill."

"Ben, I stabbed Boyd with the harpoon."

"I wondered why he was rolling around on the driveway, moaning and groaning. Where's Vivian?"

"I don't know."

They reached the driveway and saw that the first fire truck had arrived. Boyd was now propped up against the Mercedes, being ministered to by a firefighter. Sarah couldn't see the harpoon, but from the curses and groans coming from Boyd it was clear he was not mortally wounded.

Ben had parked his van behind the Mercedes. He put Emma on the back seat and then helped Harriet in beside her. "Sarah, can you drive down to my place? We need to get the police up here and tell them what happened."

Sarah nodded and climbed into the driver's seat. Her body ached from head to toe and she couldn't seem to stop her arms and hands from twitching uncontrollably. She gripped the steering wheel to steady herself. After all, it wasn't far to Ben's place. They would be safe there.

IT WAS THE FOLLOWING DAY before Vivian's burned remains were discovered in the blackened skeleton of Cliff House.

Investigators suspected that in spreading gasoline to start the blaze she had spilled some on her clothing, which had ignited.

Detective Elliot apologized to Sarah profusely.

Several days later, after her fingerprints were checked from previous prison records, it was determined that Vivian had been in Dr. Mark Lasiter's room on the day he was murdered.

By that time, Sarah knew that Vivian and Boyd had kept Harriet and Emma locked in a closet in the house on Dolphin Drive, except for the times Harriet was forced to make phone calls under the threat of harm to the child.

Boyd was arrested. The litany of charges included suspicion of kidnapping, violation of parole, vehicle theft and credit card fraud. Within days accomplice to murder was added to the charges when morphine and other narcotics were found among his possessions.

Chapter Twenty-Five

Two years later

In the dream Sarah felt Ben's lips meet hers and she slipped her arms around his neck and held him close. His hands traveled tenderly over the contours of her body and everywhere he touched her nerve endings tingled.

She gloried in the feeling of his skin against hers, of their breath mingling, and the sweet blending of their mouths as they kissed and whispered their passion and love. This was a dearly familiar path along which they traveled, savoring pleasures beyond imagining, and made safe by the certain knowledge of their love and trust.

Their bodies fused, moving in ancient rhythms. There was no time or space, they were soaring toward a rendezvous on the far side of the cosmos, and reaching it, they clung breathlessly to each other and were again astonished at the powerful force that united them, because it was not only of the flesh, but also of the mind, and something much more mysterious.

Floating dreamily back to earth, Sarah sighed contentedly.

She opened her eyes. She was nestled in the crook of Ben's arm, her hand lying on his bare chest.

He was smiling at her. "Good morning, Mrs. Travis."

"I love you, Ben," she said huskily.

"And I love you, more and more each day. I was only half-alive before you came into my life, Sarah. You know, I was lying here, watching you sleep and thinking how lucky I am."

"Oh, Ben, I love falling asleep in your arms, waking up with you beside me. I even dream about you."

He bent and kissed her. "I hope that's why you were making those very enticing murmuring sounds."

Sarah laughed and rolled over on top of him, and he stirred against her and enfolded her in his arms. He made love to her tenderly, and the reality was even more wondrous than her dream. They reached a breathtaking zenith and then, sated, drifted languorously back to a rosy anticipation of the coming day.

Sarah murmured, "What time is it? I should go and see if Emma is awake."

"No need." Ben slipped out of bed and opened the window blinds, revealing a stretch of white sand against a backdrop of sparkling blue, surf-fringed ocean. The morning sun glinted in Emma's honey-colored curls as she darted excitedly after the retreating waves. Standing hip-deep in the water, Ben's father kept one eye on the little girl and one on his fishing line.

Ben looked at Sarah, "Dad and Emma really hit it off, don't they? I think they're kindred souls when it comes to loving sand and surf. When it's low tide, he's going to start teaching her how to use a kid-size body board he bought for her."

Sarah propped herself up on one elbow to watch. She smiled fondly, trying to remember the traumatized, withdrawn child with whom she had fled from Cliff House.

"It's hard to believe she's the same little girl she was two years ago."

"You worked wonders with her, Sarah."

"Not just me!" Sarah protested. "You were so patient and understanding, and Harriet was great, too—staying with us for months when she really wanted to go back East."

"I'm still not sure that Harriet approves of me. Even though she agreed to let us adopt Emma."

"It's just her manner, Ben. Harriet is rather reserved. Besides, she knew that at her age she couldn't take care of Emma, and there was no one else. I'm amazed Harriet held up as well as she has, considering. She was so brave that night Vivian tried to burn us alive."

"You both performed some pretty remarkable feats that night, Sarah. I still get chills when I think of what that madwoman did...the lengths to which she went. Checking on you and finding out about the fire that killed your parents and fiancé. Even worming out of Harriet that my father lived in San Diego, so she could get me out of the way."

"I wish Boyd would have confessed what they did with the real Mae Peterson, so there would have been some resolution for her family."

"She's buried in the desert somewhere. No doubt in my mind. And he was convicted of killing Henry Peterson after the criminalists found blood with his DNA on Boyd's clothes."

"Well, at least we know Vivian won't hurt anyone else, and Boyd will spend the rest of his life in prison. But let's not spoil the day by remembering the evil. We've got too much to look forward to. I can't wait to tell Emma the news. I thought we'd tell her this morning. Before Harriet arrives."

"What time is her plane due?"

"Noon at Lindbergh Field."

"I wonder how the proper Long Island matron and my laid-back old man will get along?" Ben mused.

"Except for you, darling, your father is the most charming, generous, gregarious man I've ever known. Harriet is going to be completely disarmed by him."

"How did she take the news that we've decided to stay here?"

"She said that since I have a contract for my children's book, we should move to New York, closer to publishers and editors. She even offered us her house, and said she was ready for a nice apartment in town."

Ben grinned. "She sounds like Dad. What did you tell her?"

"That I love it here and so does Emma, and that it was a new start for both of us, away from sad memories. That was when Harriet agreed to come for a visit."

"I wish our house was ready."

Sarah nibbled his ear. "We'll show her the foundation."

"She'll think I'm a stereotypical Californian." He chuckled. "The only progress we've made on the house is the foundation slab, but the patio is complete with a fountain and a school of bronze flying fish."

Sarah laughed. "No, she'll think as I do, that you're the most talented artist who ever lived. Besides, how many commissions have your flying fish brought so far? Listen, Ben, if you start to feel intimidated by Harriet, just think of her shimmying down knotted bedsheets!"

He arched his eyebrows. "She sure was one gutsy old lady."

"Don't ever tell her that!"

Sarah slipped out of bed, and as she stood up Ben tenderly caressed her abdomen, then planted a kiss just above her navel. "Now let's go and tell Emma she's going to have a little brother or sister...and get ready for Dad to turn cartwheels when he hears we're going to present him with another grandchild."

They stood close together in the sunlight, savoring the perfection of the morning.